Enid Blyton®

THE SECRET SEVEN

COLLECTION 5

SHOCK FOR THE SECRET SEVEN

LOOK OUT, SECRET SEVEN

FUN FOR THE SECRET SEVEN

Illustrated by
Burgess Sharrocks

Hodder Children's Books

HODDER CHILDREN'S BOOKS

Shock for the Secret Seven first published in Great Britain in 1961 by Brockhampton Press
Look Out, Secret Seven first published in Great Britain in 1962 by Brockhampton Press
Fun for the Secret Seven first published in Great Britain in 1963 by Brockhampton Press
This collection published in Great Britain in 2017 by Hodder and Stoughton

3 5 7 9 10 8 6 4

A CIP catalogue record for this book is available from the British Library.

ISBN 978 1 444 94057 2

Typeset in Times by Avon DataSet Ltd, Bidford-on-Avon, Warwickshire

Printed and bound in Great Britain by Clays Ltd, Elcograf S.p.A.

The paper and board used in this book are made from wood from responsible sources

Hodder Children's Books
An imprint of
Hachette Children's Group
Part of Hodder and Stoughton
Carmelite House
50 Victoria Embankment
London EC4Y 0DZ

An Hachette UK Company
www.hachette.co.uk
www.hachettechildrens.co.uk

Shock for the Secret Seven

Contents

CHAPTER ONE

Secret Seven meeting, everyone!

'WHEN ARE you having a meeting of the Secret Seven again?' asked Peter's mother.

'I don't know. Why, Mother?' asked Peter, looking up from his book.

'Well, because if you do, I don't think you ought to meet in that old shed of yours,' said

his mother. 'It's such very cold weather. You'd better meet up here in the house.'

'Oh *no*, Mother,' said Janet, joining in. 'It wouldn't be a *secret* meeting then. We *must* meet in the shed.'

'Well – you'll have to heat it up a little then,' said Mother. 'I can't have you down with colds just at the end of the Christmas term. Can't you do without meetings till after Christmas?'

'Not very well,' said Janet. 'We'd half thought it would be a good idea to take the Christmas presents we're making down to the shed – all seven of us, I mean – and have a sort of Making Presents meeting. We thought we could all wear our coats.'

'You'd be frozen!' said Mother. 'I'll lend you my new little Safety-First stove – even if it's knocked over, it's safe! Then I shan't be afraid of the shed catching fire.'

'Oh, *thank* you, Mother!' said both children together, and Scamper the golden spaniel barked loudly, as if he thoroughly agreed. Janet grinned. 'He say's *he'll* be jolly glad of a stove too,' she said. 'He's a real old lie-by-the-fire these days – aren't you, Scamper?'

'Well, you should take him for a good long walk,' said Mother. 'He'd love that. You're getting fat and lazy, you two!'

She went out of the room, and Janet and Peter looked at one another. 'What with exams and one thing and another we haven't really had much time for the Secret Seven,' said Peter. 'It *would* be nice and cosy in the shed with that stove – we could take all the Christmas things we're making, and do them down there – and not have to keep taking them off the table just because meals have to be laid.'

'We'll tell the others tomorrow,' said Janet, happily. 'We shall have to have a new password – it's so long since we had a meeting. What shall we have?'

'Custard pudding!' said Peter, grinning.

'What an idiotic password!' said Janet. 'Why not ham and eggs? Or toad-in-the-hole – or . . .'

'*Toad-in-the-Hole* – that's rather a good one!' said Peter. 'It'll make the others laugh. Well done, old girl!'

'Don't call me "old girl",' said Janet. 'I keep

on telling you not to. You sound like Uncle Bertie. He always calls Auntie “old girl”.’

‘All right, young girl,’ said Peter. ‘Toad-in-the-Hole – ha, nobody will forget that! Let’s see – that’s sausage in batter pudding, isn’t it?’

‘Of course it is!’ said Janet. ‘How can you forget that, seeing that last time we had it, you ate four “toads” – four sausages – and felt rather sick afterwards.’

‘So I did,’ said Peter. ‘Scamper – the password is Toad-in-the-Hole. Don’t forget!’

‘Wuff!’ said Scamper, and wagged his tail.

Next day at school Peter called Colin, Jack and George into a corner. ‘Secret Seven meeting on Saturday at ten o’clock in the shed,’ he said. ‘The password is “Toad-in-the-Hole”. You know – sausages in batter.’

‘What a password!’ said Jack. ‘I’ll never remember such a silly one. I’ll have to write it down.’

‘No, don’t. That awful sister of yours, Susie, might find your notebook and see the password,’ said Peter.

‘All right. I’ll try and keep it in my head. I’ll make up a rhyme about it – that’ll help me to remember it,' said Jack. 'Let's see – Old King Cole was a jolly old soul, his favourite dinner was "Toad-in-the-Hole!" Ha – I'll remember it all right now.'

'You heard the time of the meeting, didn't you?' said Peter. 'You look a bit scatty this morning.'

'Well, I feel it,' said Jack. 'What with exams and things – and preparing for old Bony – he's coming to stay with me, you know – and . . .'

'Old *Bony* – who on earth is he – a skeleton or something?' asked Peter, with much interest.

'Idiot! He's a French boy – the one I went to stay with in France last year,' said Jack. 'His name is Jean Bonaparte – no relation of the great general! He's – well, he's awfully serious and earnest, and I can't say I'm much looking forward to his coming. I'm hoping Susie will like him and take him off my hands. She rather fancies herself with foreigners.'

'Don't you tell Susie anything about the meeting on Saturday,' said Peter. 'You pack her off somewhere with Bony.'

'I suppose you wouldn't let me take him to the meeting?' asked Jack, not looking very

hopeful. 'I mean – Mother's sure to say I can't leave him alone on Saturday – he's coming on Friday, you see, and it will look a bit rude to rush off by myself the very next morning.'

'You don't seem very *keen* on coming to a Secret Seven meeting,' said Peter.

'Don't be an idiot! Of *course* I want to come – but my mother isn't like yours. She doesn't think the Secret Seven is at all important. But I WILL come if I possibly can,' said poor Jack, looking scattier than ever.

'All right. But don't you let Susie know, now – and DON'T tell her the password,' said Peter, sternly. 'I hope you've not forgotten how she and Binkie, that awful giggling friend of hers, once got into our shed before a meeting, and locked the door on the inside so that *we* couldn't get in – and asked us for the password!'

Jack gave a sudden grin. 'Yes. It was *awful* of them – but honestly it had its funny side. All right – I won't give our meeting away. Trust me! I'll come somehow, even if I have to park Bony in an ice-cream shop and buy him half a dozen ices to keep him quiet! By the way, tell me the password again, Peter.'

But Peter had gone. Bother – what *was* that password now – Old King Cole? Sausages? Dinner-time? Jack went off frowning. What with his sister Susie, and exams, and Christmas looming up, *and* that stupid Bony, life was very, very difficult!

CHAPTER TWO

Password, please!

WHEN SATURDAY morning came, Peter and Janet were very busy. They carried the Safety-First stove down to the shed, and the gardener came in to light it for them. He looked round the shed.

'Ha – you've let it get pretty messy, haven't you?' he said. 'Wants a good clean, that's what it wants. Waste of a good shed, this, that's what *I* think.'

'It *isn't* wasted,' said Peter. 'We use it for our meetings. You know we do.'

'Fat lot of meetings you've had lately,' said the gardener, grumpily. 'Last month I wanted this shed for my onions, and what happened? No sooner did I put them in than I had to take them out – because you wanted it for a meeting!'

'*We* took them out, not *you*!' said Janet, indignantly. 'You didn't have to move a single one!'

The gardener gave one of his grunts, and walked out. Scamper stared after him, his tail down.

'Cheer up, Scamper,' said Janet. 'The gardener always thinks this shed is his, not ours. Peter, let's make him something for Christmas – he's not a bad sort really, though he *is* grumpy. Remember how he gave us apples to store in the shed in the autumn?'

'Yes. But we've eaten them all,' said Peter, looking hopefully up to a shelf. 'No – there's one left, all brown and shrivelled. Hey – doesn't that stove make the shed nice and warm? Hurry up and tidy round, Janet. I'll put out the boxes to sit on. Did you remember your badge? Oh, yes – you're wearing it. I hope the others will all remember theirs.'

'Wuff-wuff!' said Scamper.

'All right. I know you've lost yours, scrabbling after rabbits,' said Peter. 'Janet will make you another one when she has time.'

'Wuff!' said Scamper, again, and lay down by the stove, his tail wagging just a little. He was looking forward to seeing all the Secret Seven again!

'Almost ten o'clock,' said Peter, looking at his watch. 'Now – are the others going to be late?'

They sat down on the boxes to wait for them. The door, with its big S.S. on it, was fast shut. Footsteps came up to it at last, and someone knocked loudly.

'Peter – what's the password?' whispered Janet, suddenly. 'Was it – was it Sausages?'

'Be quiet,' said Peter, and then yelled out loudly to the knocker. 'Password, please!' Jack's voice answered.

'Peter, I've forgotten it. I just know it had something to do with dinner. Is it Roast Beef?'

'No.'

'Well – is it Fried Bacon and Eggs?'

'No. Go home if you can't remember it.'

Janet nudged Peter. '*I* forgot it, too, you know. Let him in!'

'Against the rules!' said Peter, sternly.

'Well – is it Old King Cole?' asked poor Jack.

'No, it is NOT!' said Peter. Then more footsteps were heard, and Peter called out again. 'Password, please.'

'Toad-in-the-Hole!' came the answer in a girl's voice. Peter swung open the door – and in stepped Susie, Jack's sister, with a very skinny-looking boy behind her!

'SUSIE! Get out! You don't belong to the Secret Seven! How did you know the password?' shouted Peter, very angry indeed.

'I heard Jack saying it over and over to himself two days ago,' said Susie, smiling wickedly. 'And . . .'

'Jack – you gave our password away – and you told Susie about our meeting!' cried Peter, in a great fury.

At that moment all the others came up in a bunch, and stood amazed at the sight of a furious Peter at the door of the shed, a white-faced Jack, a grinning Susie, and a skinny boy they didn't know!

'What's up?' said George. 'And who's this? A new member?' He looked at Bony, who gazed back at him owlishly through big glasses.

'My name is Jean Baptiste Bonaparte,' said the French boy, and smiled politely. 'I stay with my good friend, Jacques. His good sister, she bring me here. I thank you.'

There was a short silence. Nobody knew quite what to say. Then Colin spoke up. 'Look, I don't really know what's going on, but for goodness' sake ask us into the shed, Peter – it's freezing out here. I can't even *feel* my nose!'

Everyone surged into the shed without waiting

for an invitation – Susie and the French boy too! That was too much for Peter.

'Look here – this is supposed to be a secret meeting!' he shouted. 'Susie, get out and take Bony or Skinny or whatever his name is, with you. Go on – you don't belong to the Secret Seven.'

'Well – I'm afraid my mother will be *most* annoyed about this,' said Susie, her nose well up in the air. 'When Jack told her he couldn't play with Bony because you had said he must come to the meeting, Mother said all right, he could go, but he must take Bony too. He wouldn't take him – so *I've* brought him.'

'Well, you just take him away again!' said Peter. 'Do you hear? TAKE HIM AWAY. And you can go too, Jack.'

'No!' said Janet, at once. 'You're to stay, Jack. You're a Secret Seven member. STAY!'

CHAPTER THREE

Peter loses his temper

THE POOR French boy looked scared to death, and hurriedly backed away down the path to the front gate, bowing most politely all the time. Susie went with him, apologising to him at the top of her voice, so that all the others could hear.

'I'm so sorry, Bony, but I'm afraid Peter has *no* manners at all. You really *must* excuse him, he's never *really* learnt how to behave!'

'I'd better go with them,' said poor Jack. But Peter pulled him into the shed and banged the door so violently that the noise made Scamper leap up and bark loudly.

'Now don't *you* begin being a nuisance!' said Peter to him, in such a loud voice that Scamper

crept away, scared. Then Peter turned on Jack.

'How DARE you let Susie know the password? How *dare* you let anyone know we'd a meeting here today? And WHY aren't you wearing your badge? You don't DESERVE to be a member of the Secret Seven! And FANCY bringing that awful boy here!'

'I *didn't* bring him here. Susie did,' said poor Jack. 'And how was *I* to know she was listening at the door of my bedroom when I was trying to learn the password by saying it over and over to myself? And I *haven't* forgotten my badge. I didn't wear it in case Susie saw it and followed me. She always knows I'm going to a Secret Seven meeting when I put on my badge. Look, I've got it here in my pocket! Anyway, I had to tell Mother I was going – she wanted to know why I couldn't play with Bony. And don't you glare at me like that!'

'I'll glare at you all I like!' said Peter. 'I tell you, you don't deserve to be . . .'

'All right, all right. You've said that already,' said Jack, glaring back. 'If I don't *deserve* to belong, I *won't* belong! I'll resign! I'll walk out! Here's my badge – take it, or I'll throw it away. I don't want it any more. I can't HELP having a sister like Susie, can I? Well – now you can be the Secret SIX! Goodbye!'

He took his badge out of his pocket and threw it down at Peter's feet. Then he walked out of the door, his head high, ashamed of the sudden tears that came to his eyes. To leave the Secret Seven was the hardest thing Jack had ever done in his life!

Nobody stirred. They were all too shocked by Jack's sudden and surprising outburst. Peter stared at the fallen badge, not knowing what to do or say.

But Scamper knew what to do! He tore out of the door, barking as if to say 'Come back! Come back!' He ran round Jack's feet, and leapt up to lick him. But Jack pushed him away.

'No. Get down. You're not my friends any more.'

Scamper ran back to the shed, with his tail well down. He looked round at the others with big brown eyes, hurt and bewildered. Janet put her arm round him, and turned to her brother.

'Peter. You aren't going to let Jack go, are you? You *know* it wasn't his fault.'

Barbara suddenly burst into tears, and began to sob loudly. Peter stared at her angrily.

'Oh, don't be such a baby, Barbara, for goodness' sake! I'll ask Jack to come back, of course – but he shouldn't have lost his temper like that.'

'You lost yours,' sobbed Barbara. 'This is the f-f-f-first t-t-t-time we've ever qu-qu-qu-quarrelled. I don't l-l-like it.'

'Let's write a note to Jack,' said Colin. 'Let's tell him we can't do without him. Let's say we're sorry. Come on, Peter. You did go on at him, you know – and honestly, it's not his fault that . . .'

'I *know* it's not his fault that his sister is such a nuisance,' said Peter, who was now feeling

very uncomfortable indeed. 'All right, we'll write a note – at least, *I'll* write it, and we can all sign it. Will that do? I'm sorry I lost my temper, I really am – but Susie's enough to make anyone see red. Fancy having the nerve to bring that skinny fellow, Bony, to a Secret Seven meeting, too.'

'She simply isn't afraid of anything or anybody,' said Pam. 'It's a pity really she doesn't belong to the Secret Seven, she's really very clever, you know, and . . .'

'Belong to the *Secret Seven*!' said Peter, exploding again. 'What a thing to say, Pam! Just shut up if you can't think of anything better to say!'

'There you go again – losing your temper!' said Barbara, sticking up for Pam. 'Come on now, Peter – what about that letter to Jack? Let's do it now. I wouldn't be able to sleep tonight if I thought poor old Jack didn't belong to the Secret Seven any more.'

Peter sent Janet to the house to fetch some writing-paper. He felt ashamed of himself. He hadn't *meant* to say all that to Jack – but that Susie, that awful sister of his – well, he'd better not think of her any more, or he'd lose his temper all over again!

Soon Janet was back with writing-paper and an envelope. Solemnly they discussed what to say. In the end Peter wrote a short and apologetic note, signed by everyone.

He read it out to the others.

'*Dear Jack,*

'*Please don't let's make mountains out of mole-hills. I'm awfully sorry for what I said. You know we can't do without you! We can't* POSSIBLY *be the Secret Six. We're meeting again tomorrow evening, at six. Please come.*

I'm enclosing your badge. We ALL *want you back.*

'*From*

'PETER, JANET, PAM, BARBARA, COLIN, GEORGE.'

'Sounds all right,' said George. 'I bet he'll be glad to get it.'

'Scamper must sign it too,' said Janet. She rubbed some ink on the underneath of the spaniel's paw, and pressed it down on the paper, under their own signatures.

'There!' she said. 'Jack will know that Scamper agrees about this too. Peter, who's going to take the note? It ought to go at once.'

'I'll take it,' offered George. 'I go by his house. I'll drop it in.'

'Well, be careful Susie isn't lying in wait for you,' said Peter, licking the envelope. 'Here you are – and remember, everyone – meet here tomorrow evening at six o'clock. The password had better be the same as today, as Jack won't know any new one – and I daren't put one in this note, in case Susie gets hold of it.

Remember now – Toad-in-the-Hole!'

'Right,' said George, and took the note. 'Let's hope we'll be the Secret Seven again tomorrow!'

CHAPTER FOUR

A shock for the Secret Six

THE NEXT evening, which was Sunday, Janet and Peter went down to the shed again. Peter was a little subdued, and quite determined to be as good-tempered as Janet always was. They set the shed in order, and Janet put some little chocolate buns on a plate – a present from her mother.

'Mother doesn't know a thing about the quarrel,' she said, 'and I hope no one ever tells her. She's rather surprised we're holding another meeting so soon, though!'

'Scamper, sit down,' said Peter. 'You seem very restless tonight.'

'I think he's remembering how you and Jack shouted at one another yesterday,' said Janet.

'He's not used to us quarrelling. I think he was quite scared.'

'Silly old Scamper,' said Peter, and patted the soft, silky head. 'DEAR old Scamper – what should we do without you?'

Bang-bang! That was someone at the door already – yes, Pam and Barbara together. They whispered the password through the door. 'Toad-in-the-Hole.'

The door opened and they went in, beaming. 'Aren't we nice and early? Hasn't Jack come yet?'

'No. Not yet,' said Janet. 'Perhaps he'll come next!'

But no – George and Colin came next – knocking loudly at the door, and saying the password together. Peter opened it.

'Oh – I hoped Jack would be with you,' he said. 'He's not here yet. Well – it's not *quite* six o'clock. He'll be along in a minute. Find a box and sit down.'

Somehow they all felt rather nervous of facing Jack. They patted Scamper and talked about Christmas, and all of them listened for Jack's footsteps.

'Ah – there he is!' said Peter, as the patter of feet was heard at last. 'Toad-in-the-Hole' said a voice outside the door. Peter swung it open, beaming.

But it wasn't Jack! It was *Susie*! Her voice and Jack's were very much alike! She stood there, stern-faced, and thrust a note at Peter.

'Here you are,' she said. 'Read this. You deserve all it says!'

She pushed at the note into Peter's hand and disappeared at once into the darkness. Peter shut the door, feeling a little dazed. 'I'll open it,' he said, and slit the envelope.

'Read it out,' said Colin. And Peter, his voice shaking a little, read it to the others.

'*Dear Secret Six,*

'*Thank you for your note and apology from Peter. Sorry, but there's nothing doing. I've finished with you. I'm forming a club with Susie, Binkie, Bony and three others* – we'll *be the Secret Seven – and* you'll *be the Secret Six.*

'JACK.'

There was absolute silence after Peter had finished reading the note. Nobody knew what to say. Nobody particularly *wanted* to say anything. They sat staring at one another in such a peculiar silence that Scamper became scared.

He crept over to Janet and put his nose into her hand. She broke the silence with a sudden sob. 'Oh, Scamper – do *you* feel miserable, too, like us?'

'Peter! Peter! Jack can't mean it!' said George, finding his voice. 'He *can't* want to make a Secret Seven club with Susie and Binkie and Bony – and – who else? What shall we DO?'

'Get someone else in so that *our* club is *still* the Secret Seven!' said Peter. He crumpled up

Jack's letter. 'Jack doesn't care tuppence about us. I bet he's glad to leave us and make a new Secret Seven. But *why* did he have to call it the *Secret Seven*? He knows – he knows that's *our* special name!'

'Well – we can't have *two* Secret Seven clubs going,' said George. '*We'd* better be the Secret Six – what's it matter if we're Seven or Six? And the letters S.S. will do for Secret Six badges just as well as for Secret Seven. We shan't need to alter them.'

'Put it to the vote,' said Colin. 'We've got to do something about it, or else break up the club altogether.'

The idea of breaking up was too much for anyone. 'We'll vote!' said the girls, and the boys agreed. So very solemnly they voted and agreed that their club was now the Secret Six.

'Let's not go on with this meeting tonight,' said Janet. 'It doesn't seem right without old Jack. Let's break it up, and meet again some other time.'

Some other time? When would that be? Nobody said anything about another meeting, and day after day went by, and the Secret

Six did not meet at all. Peter's mother was surprised.

'Aren't the Secret Seven meeting again soon?' she asked. 'I hope you haven't quarrelled!'

'Oh, I expect we'll meet again *after* Christmas, Mother,' said Peter, going very red. 'You see – well – we're all pretty busy now!'

Susie was busy too! She had told her friend Binkie all that had happened, and how Jack had left the Secret Seven. 'So *we'll* be the Secret Seven!' she said. 'You and I and Jack – that's three – and Bony, his French friend – that's four – and we'll choose three others. Don't look so miserable, Jack – we'll back you up. You shall be the leader!'

At first, Jack, feeling bitter about the quarrel, agreed with everything they said – but when he found that the extra three were all to be girls, he shook his head.

'No,' he said. 'I've changed my mind. I don't want to belong to any more clubs. The Secret Seven was a fine club, and there couldn't ever be a better one. I don't want to be in another club. Don't worry about it, Susie.'

'WELL!' said Susie, in a fine rage. 'After all our sympathy, and all we've done for you, you just turn round and say "No thank you; I've changed my mind." All right then – we jolly well won't have you in our club! You can just be on your own!'

CHAPTER FIVE

Matt the shepherd has some news

CHRISTMAS CAME and went, with all its excitements and parties and pantomimes. Peter's mother came to him with a wonderful idea in the New Year.

'Would you like me to give a party for the Secret Seven?' she said. 'Just for you seven? You've had so many good times together, so many adventures – I'd love to give a grand party just for you!'

At first Peter and Janet felt thrilled – and then they remembered that they were only six. How could they explain that to Mother? She wouldn't approve at all. In fact, she would probably be very cross to think that Peter had been the cause of Jack leaving the Secret Seven.

'She might go round to Jack's mother about it,' said Peter, gloomily. 'And you know what it is when mothers get together. You never know *what* they will make you do.'

'Well, let's ask her to put off the club party till *after* the Christmas holidays,' said Janet. 'After all, we *do* have a lot of parties and things to go to.'

So, to their mother's surprise, they said please could they wait till after the holidays before they gave a party for the club? She nodded her head at once. 'Just as you like, dears,' she said. 'I don't mind *when* you have it!'

It snowed in the New Year, and Peter and Janet and Scamper were delighted. 'Lovely!' said Janet, looking out of the window at the great smooth layer of whiteness covering the farm-fields. 'LOVELY! We can go tobogganing soon. Scamper, do you hear that? Do you remember how we took you tobogganing once and you fell over and rolled all the way down the hill in the snow, collecting it round you as you went, ending up as an enormous snowball?'

'Wuff!' said Scamper, wagging his tail. He

ran to the door and pawed at it. Janet was just about to turn away from the window when she saw someone coming up the path that led to the kitchen door.

'Hello – here's Matt the shepherd,' she said. 'He looks pretty grim. I wonder what's happened? I hope there's nothing wrong with Dad's sheep, out on the snowy hills.'

Mother popped her head round the door. 'Matt the shepherd wants a word with your father,' she said. 'Find him for me, will you?'

'He's up in one of the attics, looking for something,' said Janet, and raced upstairs. 'Dad! Dad, old Matt wants you. He's at the kitchen door.'

'Now what does *he* want?' said her father. 'I only saw him yesterday, up on the hills. I'll be down in a minute, tell him.'

Janet ran downstairs and along the stone passage to the kitchen door. Matt was still standing there, his face looking very grim indeed. He didn't even smile when he saw Janet, though he was very fond of her.

'Matt! Dad's coming,' said Janet. 'Matt,

where's Shadow, your old sheep-dog? Have you left him to guard the sheep? I do like him so!'

Matt didn't say a word. Janet's father came along then, and Matt touched his hat to him, looking rather anxious.

'What is it, Matt?' asked Janet's father. 'Nothing wrong, I hope?'

'Yes, there is. Something VERY wrong,' said Matt, and to Janet's horror, she heard his voice trembling. 'You know my old friend, Shadow – my dog – my fine old collie that's won so many prizes? Well, he's gone. GONE!'

'*Gone?* What on earth do you mean?' said Janet's father. 'Not dead, surely – he wasn't more than five, was he?'

'No. He's been stolen. I'm sure of it. Shadow would never go far from me, except when he was rounding up the sheep. He's just GONE, GONE! I've whistled and called till the sheep all thought I was mad, and ran away from me – but Shadow didn't come. I – I didn't know what to do, so I came to you. I can't do without that dog of mine. He's like a brother to me, not just a dog.'

Janet felt the tears come to her eyes. She looked round for Scamper. Ah, there he was, sitting at the end of the stone passage. How dreadful it would be to be without *him*. Poor Matt! No wonder he had walked a mile or two over the snow to tell her father about his dog.

Janet's mother came to see what was the matter and soon the whole family, and Matt as well, were sitting in the living-room, discussing Shadow the collie.

Matt was terribly upset, and quite certain that his dog was stolen. 'That dog of mine's worth a whole lot of money!' he said. 'The prizes he wins! I could sell him for a thousand pounds, but I wouldn't take a thousand for him. No, that I wouldn't. The times he's sat all night beside me when I've been tending the sheep – the times when he's run for miles to find a lost one, and come back laughing all over his face! He could laugh, that dog could. I never had a dog that was better company.'

They all let the old shepherd talk and talk. It seemed to help him – but at the end there was a deep silence. Matt twisted his hat round and round in his horny brown hands, that could be so tender with the tiny, new-born lambs, and looked at Janet's mother so mournfully that she felt she too would cry, just as Janet was doing!

'Don't you worry, Matt,' said Janet's father at last. 'I'll get straight on to the police. You're quite certain he couldn't have wandered away and lost himself?'

'What! A hill-born collie that's kept my sheep for years?' said Matt, scornfully. 'Best collie-dog I ever had too. Like a brother, he was. I *must* have him back. I'll not stay on these hills without him. I'd fret too much.'

'Right, Matt. You go back to your sheep, and I'll telephone the police right away,' said Janet's father. 'Don't worry too much. Why – you may find old Shadow waiting up there for you!'

'Well, if I do – and dear knows I hope you're right – I'll stand at the top of the hill there and wave my old cloak,' said Matt, and went slowly back to the kitchen door, and away over the snow.

'Oh, *Mother*!' said Janet, 'will he get Shadow back again?'

'I hope so,' said her mother. 'But if it's a dog-stealer at work, it may be very difficult.'

'Mother – will *Scamper* be all right?' said

Peter, and a feeling of sudden dread went through him. 'Mother, Scamper is valuable, isn't he – a pedigree golden spaniel?'

'Yes. Yes, he is,' said his mother. 'But I don't think you need worry, dear – it would be very difficult to steal a dog living in a household, one who is under our eyes all the time. Shadow was always off and away over the hills for miles, you know. If anyone liked to tempt him with a bit of meat, he might take it, and be captured.'

'I felt so sorry for old Matt,' said Peter sadly. 'Scamper – where are you? For goodness' sake keep near us all day long – and you'd better be sure to sleep in my room at night too – and . . .'

'Oh, come now – you really needn't worry about Scamper,' said his mother. 'He would NEVER go off with a stranger.'

'Here comes Pam,' said Janet, looking out of the window. 'Goodness – she looks as miserable as old Matt. What can be the matter with *her*? Oh, I do hope she hasn't bad news too!'

They heard Pam's voice calling them. 'Janet – Peter – something dreadful's happened. Let me in quickly!'

CHAPTER SIX

Warning – dog-stealer about!

PETER RACED to the front door and opened it. 'What's the matter, Pam? What's happened?'

'Oh, Peter – you know my granny? You know her lovely poodle – the white one that always looks as if it has a coat of snow? Well, it's been stolen! And, oh, Peter, I thought perhaps we could have a meeting about it, and see if the Secret Seven – I mean the Secret Six – can do anything to help? Granny's so upset!'

'Goodness gracious!' said Peter, pulling Pam indoors. 'We've only just heard that somebody has stolen our shepherd's dog, Shadow! He was very valuable, too. It must be the same thief. Quick – come and tell my father. He's just going to telephone the police about Shadow.'

Pam went into the living-room with Peter, still crying. She loved Snowy the poodle and had taken him for many a walk. Now he was gone! Would they ever get him back?

'Daddy, wait a minute – don't telephone the police yet. Another dog's been stolen!' said Peter, rushing up to his father. 'Pam, tell my father about Snowy.'

Pam sobbed out all she knew. 'My granny let him out last night, about nine o'clock, as she always does – and when she called him, he didn't come in! She called and whistled and then put on a coat to look for him. But all she saw was – was – boo-hoo-hoo – was . . .'

'Was *what*?' said Peter impatiently, imagining all kinds of dreadful things.

'She saw footsteps in the snow in her garden,' sniffed Pam. 'Great BIG footprints, tramping all about. And Snowy's neat little footprints were there too – and in one place the snow was all scuffed up, as if Snowy had been dragged along. Oh, Peter, *can* the Secret Seven do anything?'

'You mean the Secret *Six*,' said Peter. 'Well, we'll certainly call a meeting about it – and about our shepherd's dog too. After all, we've solved quite a lot of mysteries – but we've never come up against a dog-stealer before. What a horrible man he must be!'

Peter's father listened to all that Pam said, frowning. It did look as if there was some professional dog-stealing going on in their district! *Two* dogs stolen now – and both valuable ones!

'I'll tell the police about Snowy, as well as about Shadow,' he said, and picked up the telephone receiver. In a few moments he was on to the police-station. The three children heard him giving all details to the police. Then they heard him say: 'What! THREE more dogs stolen, besides these two, did you say? Well, what are you going to do about it? A dog isn't just a dog, you know – it's a friend of the family.'

He put down the receiver, and turned to the listening children. 'Three valuable dogs besides Shadow and Snowy have been stolen,' he said. 'And in every case, there have been these footprints in the snow – large prints – the police think the fellow must be a tall, heavy

fellow, who knows a great deal about dogs – or who has someone behind him who knows, and who tells him where to go.'

Tears were in Janet's eyes. She was holding Scamper close to her, as if she were afraid he might be stolen at any minute! 'Oh, Daddy – can we lock Scamper up in your room? I KNOW he'll be stolen too – he's so beautiful and good and so valuable. He's a pedigree dog, isn't he?'

'Yes – and he *is* worth a lot of money,' said her father. 'I think perhaps we *had* better guard him carefully till the thief is caught. There's one thing – the thief will treat all the dogs well, because their value would go down, if they were ill or thin, and not worth selling.'

'But – but Scamper would be MISERABLE if someone took him away from us,' said Peter. 'He'd go thin at once, I know he would. And I

don't believe he'd eat a thing. What would happen to him then?'

'Let's not worry about things before they happen,' said his father. 'Look after Scamper well, and don't let him leave your side. He's well trained – he's not likely to go to any strangers at all. Now, I'm expecting the police at any moment – I have to take them up to Matt's hut so that they can find out if the footprints in the snow there are the same as the others they have found.'

'We'll go with you,' said Janet. 'And we'll

take Scamper. He ought to be all right with three people to look after him.'

'Yes, you go,' said her mother. 'The walk will do you good. Scamper – walkies, walkies!'

'Wuff!' said Scamper in delight, and flew to the door.

'Wait! Wait for us!' shouted Peter, afraid that Scamper would rush out and be stolen at once. 'Look, Mother, there's someone out in the yard – *he* might be the thief!'

'Don't be silly, dear – that's only the postman,' said his mother. 'Go and see if he has a parcel for me – I'm expecting one.'

Peter went to the door in answer to the postman's double knock. 'Hallo, postman!' he said. 'Ah – you *have* a parcel for my mother. Do I sign for it?'

'Yes, please,' said the postman, and bent down to pat Scamper. He was a little man, with a round, smiling face, and Peter and Janet liked him very much. As for Scamper, he adored him, and frisked round him, barking in delight.

'You want to be careful of this lovely dog of yours,' said the postman, patting Scamper.

'There's a dog-stealer about, you know. Old Mrs Thom's lovely dog has been taken – and Mr Cartwright's dachshund – ah, he was a beauty, he was, with a coat like silk! And Miss Downey told me this morning her little Scottie was taken last week – priceless, he was – worth goodness knows how much money! You be careful of this here spaniel of yours – don't you let any stranger feed him, or let him go off on his own.'

'We won't!' said Peter, taking Scamper by the collar. 'It would be a very, very clever thief who could get hold of our Scamper. Wouldn't it, Scamper?'

'Wuff-wuff-wuff!' said Scamper, as if he understood every single word.

CHAPTER SEVEN

Up to the hills

PETER, JANET, Pam and Scamper sat down near the fire. Pam began to cry again as she spoke about Snowy, the poodle that had belonged to her granny.

'Peter, don't you think we could call a meeting of the Seven – I mean the Six?' she said. 'I *do* want to get back Snowy, if I can, and I know I can't by myself. I'm not clever enough about finding clues, and things like that. Please, please do call a meeting.'

'All right,' said Peter. 'I will. I'll tell the others – I'll send them a note each. You and Pam can write one each, and I'll do the other. What about tomorrow morning? Now it's holidays, it would be nicer to meet in the mornings – it's so dark at night.'

So the three sat down at the table, and wrote out neat little notes – one to Barbara, one to George and one to Colin. 'IMPORTANT. *Please meet in the S.S. shed tomorrow morning at half-past ten sharp.*'

'Seems funny not to send one to Jack,' said Pam, as she licked her envelope. 'I suppose we couldn't *possibly* ask him to come?'

'No,' said Peter. 'He's probably got together another club now, and called it the Secret Seven.'

'Well, *I* don't believe he has,' said Pam. 'I met him out the other day and he looked pretty miserable. He had that funny skinny boy with him – what's his name now – Bonaparte? Bony's a really good name for him. He was talking at top speed, waving his arms about like anything, and old Jack wasn't saying a single word.'

'Don't let's talk about Jack,' said Peter. 'Now – who's going to take these notes?'

'I will – on my way home,' said Pam, getting up from the table. 'And for goodness' sake, Peter, watch over your dear old Scamper. What the Secret Seven – I mean the Secret Six – would do without him, I really don't know!'

'Scamper would never, never go with any stranger,' said Peter. 'Would you, Scamper?'

'Wuff-wuff-WUFF!' said Scamper, at once.

'He said "Certainly NOT",' said Peter, and Pam looked at Scamper admiringly.

'He really *talks*!' she said. 'Well, I must be going. I won't forget to leave the notes. See you tomorrow at half-past ten. Oh – same password as before – what was it now? It's so long since we had the last meeting.'

'Well – it's – er . . .' began Peter.

'Old King Cole,' said Janet.

'Sausages!' said Pam.

'No – Frog in the Pond!' said Janet, knowing quite well

it was not. 'Goodness – we're as bad as Jack.'

'It was Toad-in-the-Hole, as you both know very well,' said Peter, remembering. 'All right – see you tomorrow, Pam.'

Peter and Janet spent the rest of the day watching Scamper, making certain that he did not disappear anywhere. If he went out of the sitting-room into the kitchen to beg a titbit, they went too. If he went for a little run, he was put on the lead at once, and guarded every inch of the way by both Peter and Janet. If he ran into the hall when someone came to the door, they went with him. He was rather surprised, but very pleased.

'You know, Janet, I think one of the things we ought to discuss at the meeting is the report saying that the same kind of footprints are found each time the dogs were stolen,' said Peter. 'I wish we could get a picture of the footprints, so that we could see the size and shape – you never know if we *might* come across them somewhere and be able to *follow* the thief.'

'Oh, *yes*!' said Janet. 'But, Peter – won't the police be doing that?'

'Yes. But there's no reason why we shouldn't

help in any tracking, is there?' said Peter. 'Listen – who's that at the front door?'

'A policeman!' said Janet. 'I expect he's come about Matt's collie. Dad said he'd take him up to Matt's hut – don't you remember?'

'Yes – of course!' said Peter. 'Let's ask Dad if we can go with him. We might take a pencil and paper and copy any footprints we find.'

'Oh, *yes*!' said Janet. 'I'll get some paper at once – and a measuring tape. Peter, ask Dad if we can go with him.'

'Yes,' said the children's father. 'You can come. Do you good to have a walk! Put your snowboots on.'

And two minutes later Janet, Peter, their father and Cobbett the policeman all trailed up the long hill to where Matt the shepherd lived in his little hut, all among the sheep. Scamper raced with them, very happy. But Matt wasn't there.

'He's out with the sheep – looking for two or three missing ones, I expect,' said Peter's father. 'Now he's lost his sheep-dog, he's no one to help him. I must borrow another dog for him if I can. A shepherd is lost without a good dog to help him. I reckon I'll lose a lot of my sheep if his old Shadow doesn't come back.'

'Good name for a sheep-dog – Shadow,' said Cobbett. 'Now, sir – where did Matt say the dog disappeared?'

'He didn't say,' said Peter. 'He just said he'd been stolen. Hey, LOOK! Footprints! Big ones, too!'

But his father and the policeman had gone on, looking for Matt, and took no notice of Peter's excited voice. 'Where's that paper you brought, Janet?' said Peter, thrilled. 'We'll copy these prints and show them to Dad when he comes back. They might be a VERY FINE CLUE!'

CHAPTER EIGHT

Footprints in the snow

THE FOOTPRINTS were large and clear. They were right at the back of the hut, and looked as if someone had been standing about there.

'I bet this is where the thief stood while he waited to catch Shadow!' said Peter. 'Bother – I wish I had something flat to put this paper on. I can't draw properly standing up.'

'I'll measure the prints,' said Janet, feeling most important. She took out the tape-measure she had brought, and did a little measuring. She called the figures out to Peter, and he wrote them down. Then he went into the little hut to find something flat on which to put his paper, so that he could do a little sketch of the prints.

He came out with an old tray. He turned it

upside down, sat down in the snow just beside the footprints and painstakingly copied a print of a left foot and a print of a right foot. They really were very big!

'Very good!' said Janet, admiringly. 'Look, here come the others again. Let's show your drawings to them.'

Matt came slowly back with the children's father and the policeman. He looked old and sad. Janet couldn't bear to look at him. 'I hate dog-thieves, I hate dog-thieves!' she said over and over again to herself. Peter ran up to his father.

'Look!' he said. 'We found some footprints and we copied them. We found them behind Matt's shed – and we thought they must have been made by the thief when he stood out there, waiting to catch Shadow.'

The policeman took the paper at once. He looked hard at the drawings, and then he looked at Peter.

'I'm sorry, lad,' he said. 'These aren't the thief's footprints.'

'Well, whose are they, then?' said Peter, surprised.

'They belong to old Matt here,' said the policeman, with a little grin. 'Fine drawings they are, Peter – but not much use, seeing they belong to the *owner* of the dog. Take a look at Matt's prints here now in the snow – just where he's been walking. He's wearing huge old snowshoes – bigger even than the prints you've drawn – proper shepherd's boots they are, meant for all weathers.'

Sure enough, the prints Peter had drawn *had* been made by old Matt! He nodded his head when he heard where Peter had seen them. 'Ah, yes. I stand behind the hut there when I want to count my sheep down in the valley. They're my prints all right. See, there's even the place shown here, where the cobbler mended the sole with a patch! They're *my* prints, not the thief's. Ah, wait till I catch him, wait till . . .'

'All right, all right, Matt, old friend,' said Peter's father, seeing that the old man was trembling. 'Take things easy now. We'll get Shadow back, don't you worry. Now come along you two – it's probably going to snow again. We'd best get back. Matt, you come along for a hot drink at tea-time – and we'll give you some in a flask to take back with you.'

'Aye. Thank you,' said Matt, and turned away, his eyes roving the snowy hills, always on the watch for his beloved Shadow. When would he see him again, bounding lightly along, his eager eyes looking for his beloved master?

'Dad, how would a dog-thief entice old Shadow away?' asked Peter. 'He's very fierce, you know, if anyone goes near his sheep. I've seen him show all his teeth and growl in a most terrifying way if a tramp walks by. I shouldn't have thought *anyone* could steal a faithful old dog like Shadow.'

'He probably wasn't enticed,' said his father. 'It would be easy enough to throw down a piece of meat and leave it for Shadow to find and eat – meat with some kind of drug inside perhaps, that would send a dog to sleep.'

'Oh! How horrible!' said Janet. 'You mean that the thief would come back, and pick up the sleeping dog and take him away – in a car or something?'

'Yes. That's exactly what I do mean,' said her father. 'I asked old Matt if he had seen any strangers around, but he hadn't. He says nobody comes up to his hut except his friends – old Burton the hedger, for instance, who trims the hedges round the field – and sometimes the gardener goes up to him with vegetables – and his brother goes to see him – and the grocer's boy takes him goods once a week – and occasionally the postman calls – all people who are his friends, and whom he knows well.'

'A *hiker* might go up to his hut,' said Janet. '*He* might see Shadow and steal him by throwing down meat like you said.'

'Don't be silly, Janet,' said Peter. 'Shadow would fly at him if old Matt wasn't there. He wouldn't allow *any* stranger near the sheep – and anyway, who would hike round the country now that it's deep in snow? They'd get lost! Why, even we, who know the way well, could hardly follow the path up to Matt's hut.'

'All right, all right,' said Janet. 'I was only trying to think of every single idea I could. Actually there's only one thing we know for certain – and that is that there *is* a dog-stealer about!'

'Come along now,' said her father, impatiently. 'I want to get back. I've so much to do this morning. You keep your eyes open, and see if the Secret Seven can use their brains and track down this thief. You've been clever enough before. Why not have a meeting about it?'

'That's JUST what we've planned!' said Peter, bounding along over the snow. 'Tomorrow morning, Dad! We're going to put our heads together, and find that dog-thief, if it takes us *weeks* to do it! Aren't we, Scamper?'

And Scamper, of course, made his usual answer – 'WUFF!'

CHAPTER NINE

Susie, Janet – and Bony!

THE FIRST thing Janet thought of next morning when she awoke was that there was to be a Secret Seven meeting that day. 'No,' she corrected herself, 'I mean Secret *Six*! I shall never get used to being the Six instead of the Seven. Oh, I do WISH Jack still belonged. I do WISH he'd come back.'

She had to go to the town that morning to do some shopping for her mother. 'I'll go straight-away now, Mother,' she said. 'We've a meeting this morning you know, down in the shed – an important one – about the dog-stealing that's going on. Oh – that reminds me – where's Scamper? I haven't seen him for at least ten minutes!'

'He's out in the kitchen,' said her mother.

'Can't you smell his meaty bones cooking? He's always sure to be out there then! Now look, here's the list, dear. If you hurry, you will be back in good time for your meeting. Are you going to take Scamper with you?'

'Only if he's on the lead,' said Janet. 'You see, that dog-thief might be hiding somewhere, Mother, watching for really good dogs.'

'Well, I hardly think he would steal Scamper in the middle of a busy shopping morning,' said her mother. 'He won't like being on the lead. Anyway, he *never* goes to a stranger.'

All the same, Janet put the surprised Scamper on the lead, and walked off with him, the basket in her other hand. When she came by the police-

station she saw several people reading a notice on the board outside. She went up to see what it said. It was a list of dogs that had disappeared during the last few days!

'LOST, STOLEN or STRAYED' it began, and then came the names and addresses of NINE dogs!

'*Nine!*' said Janet. 'Two from the next village, and seven from ours; Scamper, keep to heel!'

She turned as someone called her name. 'Hallo, Janet! I see Scamper isn't stolen yet!'

It was Susie, Jack's sister. She was walking along with Binkie, her friend, and Bony, the French boy. Jack was not with them.

'Hallo,' said Janet, who didn't like Susie.

'How are the Secret Six?' inquired Susie. 'All well and happy, I hope?'

'I don't want to talk to you,' said Janet. 'Scamper, come to heel!'

But Scamper was straining at his lead, trying his hardest to lick the French boy's legs. Bony patted him, and Scamper went nearly mad with joy. He jumped up at him and licked his face.

'Scamper!' said Janet, in amazement. 'You've only seen Bony once, and that was for just a little while – why are you making such a fuss of him?'

'Oh, dogs *adore* Bony,' said Susie, and Binkie nodded her head. 'They go mad over him, even if they've never seen him before. *Ça, c'est vrai, mon petit, n'est ce pas*?' she added in French, turning to the French boy. He nodded.

'Oh don't show off your wonderful French in front of *me*,' said Janet. 'Scamper, stop it! You're being soppy.'

'Soppee, soppee – what is soppee?' asked the French boy, fondling Scamper's silky ears. 'He ees a *chien très beau* – how do you say?'

'Bony says he's a very beautiful dog,' translated Susie, for Janet's benefit.

'Thanks – I understand *that* much French,' said Janet. '*Will* you stop pulling, Scamper? Why on earth have you suddenly gone mad over a French boy you don't know?'

Two more dogs came bounding up just then, and stopped at once when they came to Bony. In a moment they were rubbing lovingly against him, pawing him, licking him.

'There you are!' said Susie proudly, just as if Bony was a very clever brother. 'See how they love him? It's always the same – *any* dog adores dear Bony.'

The skinny boy patted and stroked and spoke to the dogs very lovingly in quick French, which Susie pretended to understand, nodding her head wisely all the time. Binkie nodded too, and Janet suddenly felt furious.

'SCAMPER!' she shouted. 'Come away! You know you're not supposed to be friendly with strangers. You'll be stolen one of these days, if you're so silly.'

'Stolen?' said the French boy, looking alarmed. 'Ah *oui* – there is a – what you call it – a dog-thief here in this town. Jack, *mon ami*, he tell me so.'

'"*Mon ami*" means "my friend",' said Susie. 'Jack is his friend, you see.'

'Susie, stop speaking to me as if I was in the first year!' said Janet, her face red with rage. 'Scamper, WILL YOU come here!'

Scamper stopped fussing over Bony, and at once the other two dogs took his place, whining with pleasure as the boy patted them. It really *was* rather extraordinary. Bony said something rapidly in French as Janet walked off, and Susie translated, calling after her.

'Janet! Bony says Scamper's a valuable dog and you'd better take care of him if a dog-thief is around.'

'As if I didn't know *that*!' called back Janet, and marched off, head in air, swinging her shopping basket. That awful Susie! Showing off like that! And that grinning Binkie friend of hers! And what an *extraordinary* boy Bony was – so skinny, so short-sighted and owlish – and yet how fond he must be of animals for dogs to go to him like that. It just showed how silly dogs could be – *any* of those dogs – yes, even

Scamper – would have followed him for miles.

'I'll report you at our meeting this morning for behaving like that,' she said to Scamper. 'Why, if that boy wanted to steal you, you'd have let him. You are a very foolish brainless dog today, Scamper.'

Scamper put his tail down, and followed Janet meekly while she did her shopping, not daring even to pull at the lead. Why was Janet cross? Didn't she know that that boy was a dog-lover, and that every dog in the town knew it?

Janet soon finished her shopping, raced home, and looked at the clock. Was she late for the meeting? No – she had one minute to spare. She pinned on her badge and then down the garden she raced and banged at the shed door. She could hear voices inside.

'Password!' shouted Peter.

'Toad-in-the-Hole!' shouted back Janet.

The door opened, and Peter looked out crossly. 'JANET! Haven't I told you before not to yell the password at the top of your voice? Come in, idiot. You're last. We were just about to begin. Sit down. Scamper, you sit down, too, for goodness' sake, and let's begin.'

CHAPTER TEN

A really interesting meeting

THE SIX were now all ready for their meeting, Scamper too. He sat solemnly beside Peter, looking as if he might join in the conversation at any minute.

'Now, this meeting has been called at Pam's request,' he began. 'We all know why. It's about this dog-stealing business.'

'Wuff,' said Scamper, hearing the word 'dog'.

'Please don't interrupt, Scamper,' said Peter, solemnly, making Barbara give a sudden giggle. 'Pam, tell us about your granny's dog, and all details about its being stolen.'

Pam poured out the whole story, and tears began to run down her cheeks. Scamper was upset, and crept over to her, trying to lick them as they fell.

'Don't let's get upset, now,' said Peter. 'That won't do any good. We've got to discuss this subject, and see if there's anything we can do to find the thief and stop other dogs being stolen. You see – there's Scamper to think about – and all kinds of dogs in the town. And there's dear old Shadow, our shepherd's dog. We simply MUST get him back.'

'But I don't see what *we* can do!' said George. 'I mean – if the *police* can't find the thief, what chance have *we*?'

'We've solved other problems before,' said Peter. 'And anyway, children sometimes hear things and spot things that grown-ups don't. And . . .'

'But what do we *know* about the thief?' said George. 'Nothing at all! How can we find a thief we don't know anything about?'

'That's where you're wrong,' said Peter. 'We *do* know certain things about him. We know for instance that he has *very* big feet.'

'So have plenty of other people,' persisted

George. 'My father, for instance. He wears size t—'

'Oh, do shut up, George,' said Peter. '*I'm* doing the talking. You can make your comments later.'

'Ha ha!' said George, in a hollow kind of voice. 'You've gone all high and mighty now. "Make your comments!" Who's going to propose a vote of thanks today, Peter? And is anyone going to . . .'

'Oh, get out, George, if you can't listen!' said Peter, exasperated. 'Don't you understand that this is a very special meeting? It might even save old Scamper from being stolen. It might be the means of finding dear old Shadow. It might . . .'

'All right, Peter,' said George, impressed. 'Go on. I won't interrupt again.'

'I'll just briefly say what we know for certain about the thief,' said Peter. 'It's what the police told my father. They said that, judging by the big, deep footprints left in the snow by the thief – *very* large prints – the man must be a tall, heavy fellow, who knows a great deal about dogs – whether they're valuable or not, I mean.

He's stealing only pedigree dogs – ones that are valuable, and can be sold for a good price.'

'But why don't the dogs *bark* when they're stolen?' asked Colin. 'Scamper here would howl the place down if anyone tried to take him away.'

'It's likely that the thief throws down meat with some sort of sleep-drug in it,' said Peter. 'The dog eats it – falls asleep in his kennel – or on the street maybe, or garden – and then the thief picks him up and goes off with him.'

'And doesn't anybody think it's odd to see someone carrying a fast-asleep dog – a big one like Shadow the collie, for instance – fast asleep in somebody's arms – or over his shoulder!' said Janet. 'I don't believe that!'

'All right. *You* think of some way to entice a dog away without bribing him or drugging him,' said Peter.

'Well, I *do* know a way,' said Janet, making everyone sit up straight in astonishment. 'I *do* know a way. Now, believe it or not, this morning when I was out shopping, Scamper suddenly went to a COMPLETE stranger, and licked him and loved him, and didn't want to come with me even when I ordered him to.'

'I don't believe *that*!' said Peter at once. 'Whatever do you mean, Janet?'

'Just exactly what I say,' said Janet, and straightaway told the meeting what had happened when she had taken Scamper shopping with her that morning, and had met Susie and Binkie with Bony, the French boy.

'You should have *seen* Scamper!' she said. 'He went all soppy and silly over Bony, whined at him, and licked him and jumped up at him – just as if he was a long-lost friend. I was really ashamed of him. Fancy going crazy over *Bony* of all people. And not only *Scamper* behaved like that. Every dog that came by was the same. And it didn't even seem to matter to the dogs that Bony talked to them in *French*!'

There was a silence after this little speech of Janet's. Everyone stared at Scamper in the greatest astonishment. He stared back, wagging his tail a little. He knew he was being talked about, and he wasn't sure if he was going to be scolded or not.

'Sounds a bit like the story of the Pied Piper of Hamelin,' said Colin, at last. 'You remember how every single boy and girl loved him and followed him? Well, this boy Bony sounds like a Pied Piper for dogs!'

'I remember a girl at school once who was like that with cats,' said Pam. 'She had only to walk down the road and the cats would come running up to her – big ones, little ones, even kittens! They all adored her, and she adored them. It was most peculiar to watch. Even our old solemn cat, Tiddles, used to wait for her to come by, and then she'd try to jump down to the girl's shoulder, purring as loudly as a . . . as a . . .'

'Motor-bike?' said George, and that made them all laugh.

'I see what you're getting at,' said Peter. 'You think these valuable dogs might not be drugged or enticed with food, but just follow a sort of Pied Piper fellow who loves dogs so much that they can't help following him. Well, I just don't believe that. Scamper, for instance, might lick Bony all over if he *met* him – but he certainly wouldn't go *away* with him!'

'I agree with you,' said George. 'And . . .'

'Knock-knock-knock.' Someone was at the

door. Peter at once thought it must be Susie and Binkie.

'Keep out! This is a private meeting!' he shouted, fiercely.

'Well – is it too private for cups of cocoa and new-made buns?' said a familiar voice, and Peter leapt up at once.

'Mother! You pet! Just what we all felt like! Come in, do. We can continue our meeting afterwards. Ooh – what gorgeous buns! Get *down*, Scamper, or you'll have hot cocoa all over your nose. Thanks so much, Mother.'

CHAPTER ELEVEN

A shock for Peter and Janet

THE SIX, and Scamper, set to work on the hot buns and the steaming cocoa. They felt warmed and happy and cosy. The meeting was going quite well, and everyone felt rather important, discussing how they were going to help the police to find the dog-stealer. Peter passed round the sketches he had made of footprints behind old Matt's hut, and they were much admired.

'Well – to go on with our meeting,' said Peter, when every bun was eaten and every drop of cocoa drunk. 'I think we may safely rule out the idea that the dogs are stolen by a kind of Pied Piper – that is, if the dogs are anything like *Scamper* – who would certainly

NEVER follow a stranger, however much he liked him. And you must admit that *most* dogs are taught not to go with strangers, especially if they're valuable dogs.'

'Quite right,' said Pam and Colin, together.

'So we come back to the idea that somebody is throwing down food that puts a dog to sleep when he eats it. I mean – it would be a very easy thing to do, wouldn't it? For instance, take Scamper – he might be sniffing along a hedge, and find a dollop of meat just thrown down by a passer-by – the thief. He gobbles it up at once – runs a little way – drops down asleep – and up comes the thief and takes him away. If it's done at night, nobody would see.'

'I don't much like this,' said Janet, gathering Scamper up in her arms. 'It sounds too easy for words. Scamper, for goodness' sake listen carefully, and don't let it happen to *you*!'

'Well, it seems to me that the *only* thing we can do is to use the clues that the police told my father about, and look out for anyone tall, heavily made, with enormous feet,' said Peter. 'The police thought he was heavily built because the footprints they found in the snow were very deep – as if the thief was a burly, heavy man.'

'Right. Then you want us to look out for someone like that, and see if we can find out anything about him – if he goes out at night, for instance?'

'Yes,' said Peter. 'But for goodness' sake don't let anyone *know* you're following them, or snooping, or we'll get into trouble. Janet, I think Scamper wants to go out. He's scraping at the door. Stop it, Scamper! Hurry up, Janet, and let him out.'

'Had I better go out with him?' said Janet, anxiously. 'I mean – he *might* get stolen!'

'Don't be an idiot!' said Peter. 'Stolen in daylight in our own garden, with all of us here to hear him bark? Impossible!'

Janet opened the door, and Scamper disappeared, barking in delight. The meeting went on, and after everyone had promised to keep their eyes open and report anyone acting suspiciously, or looking like the thief, Peter declared the meeting closed.

'Almost twelve o'clock,' he said, looking at his watch. 'Gosh, how the time goes when we talk and talk! Well, good luck, everyone – and be sure to report anything interesting.'

He and Janet walked back to the house, Peter carrying the empty cups. 'A very good meeting, wasn't it?' he said. 'Jack's missing something interesting – I bet he wishes he hadn't walked out on us!'

'Where's Scamper?' said Janet. 'SCAMPER! SCAMPER! The meeting's over, Scamper! Here, Scamper. Here! Come along!'

No Scamper appeared, and something cold seemed suddenly to clutch at Janet's heart. She stood quite still, and looked at Peter, fear on her face. 'Peter!' she said, in a half-whisper. 'Why doesn't Scamper come? Oh, Peter . . .'

'Idiot! I suppose you think somebody came along and cleverly stole him while we sat in the shed,' said Peter. 'Just like that! Without a bark or a whimper or a howl from old Scamper. *Really*, Janet! He's probably in the kitchen, begging for a new-baked bun.'

'Yes. Yes, of course he is,' said Janet. 'I'll go and see.'

But Scamper wasn't in the kitchen. He didn't appear at all, even when Peter yelled for him in his very loudest voice. Mother came to see what all the shouting was about.

'Mother – we can't find Scamper!' said Janet, desperately. 'He slipped out towards the end of the meeting. Mother, have you seen him?'

'I haven't seen him since I came to bring you buns and cocoa,' said Mother. 'Don't look so upset, dear – he's sure to be about. He may have gone rabbiting.'

'Not in the snow, Mother,' said Janet, in a trembling voice. 'Mother, I've a *dreadful* feeling about him. He's stolen – I know he is! Oh, Mother!'

She flung herself on her mother and cried bitterly. 'Don't be *silly*, Janet!' said her mother. 'He's probably gone to meet your father.'

But he hadn't. He seemed to have completely disappeared! There was no sight or sound of him. He just simply wasn't to be found. Peter and Janet and their mother hunted everywhere, and called and whistled. No Scamper came running, with big silky ears flapping as he pattered along.

It was a very puzzled and unhappy family

that came to the table at one o'clock. The children's father was back from his walk over the farm, and hadn't seen a sign of Scamper. 'But he *can't* have been stolen,' he said for the twentieth time. 'You'd have heard him bark if he'd been taken away by anyone. Scamper would never, never go with a stranger without a great struggle. He'd bite him, he'd fly at him!'

'Not if someone gave him drugged meat and he fell asleep after he'd eaten it, and was picked up like that,' sobbed Janet. 'You know that's what probably happened to the other dogs. The police said so.'

'Now, let's think,' said her father. 'Who has been here this morning – what tradespeople have called?'

'Well, let's see now who's been here in the last hour,' said Janet's mother. 'There was the grocer with his van – and Alfred and John Higgins, two little boys collecting for something – and the postman – and the laundry-man and his van – and old Mrs Hughes, calling for the mending – and a man after a farm-job . . .'

'After a farm-job? *That* sounds like someone who might steal Scamper!' said Peter. 'Dad – Dad, can we trace him? Quick, Dad, ring up the police. We *must* get dear old Scamper back, we must, we must!'

CHAPTER TWELVE

Who can have stolen Scamper?

NOBODY EVEN thought about dinner-time – all that anyone thought of was Scamper! Where was he? Was he *really* stolen? Peter's father rang up the police at once, and asked them to keep a look-out for Scamper. 'He can't have been gone for much more than an hour!' he said.

'Stolen from your garden, you say, sir?' said the policeman. 'Have you a list of people calling at your house during the time you mention?'

'Yes – and there seems to have been quite a stream of callers – some with vans!' said Peter's father. 'A van would have been very useful. If Scamper had been popped into one, the running of the engine would have drowned his barking.'

'About this man who called for a job on the farm, sir – have you a description of him?' asked the policeman.

'Yes – I saw him myself – a little fellow with a limp. Not strong enough for farm-work.'

'Well, that rather rules him out, sir,' said the

policeman. 'We think the thief is a big fellow, you know, with big feet to match.'

'Yes – well, you're probably right,' said Peter's father.

'I think the small boys who came collecting can be dismissed as suspects too,' said the policeman. 'We'll find out about the man who came inquiring after a job – just in case, sir.'

'Right. I'll see the laundry-man and the grocer,' said Peter's father. 'I don't for one moment think they're the thieves, though – we know them so well.'

'Ah, but they've each a van. Easy enough to entice a dog into a van – slam the door – and drive off!'

That afternoon Peter and his father went to the laundry and asked to see the van-man who collected their dirty laundry that morning. He came out at once, and nodded to Peter, who had often ridden in his van when he was smaller.

'I hear you want to see me. Anything I can do?'

'Er – did you happen to see our dog Scamper when you called this morning?'

'Well, no. Don't tell me he's been stolen!'

'We're rather afraid he has,' said Peter. 'What time did you come to the house?'

'Let's see now – about quarter-past eleven, and I didn't see a sign of the dog. He usually comes up wagging his tail – very good-tempered dog.'

'Quarter-past *eleven*! Well, he was down in the shed with *us*, then!' said Peter.

'Sorry I can't help you more. I know how you feel about the dog. I'd feel the same about mine.' The man clapped Peter sympathetically on the shoulder. 'Hope you find him!'

Peter and his father went off. 'Well, it *can't* have been the *laundry*-man,' said Peter. 'I didn't think it could be. He's too nice. Let's go to the grocer's now, Dad. The grocer's man is a great big fellow – he fits the description of the thief better than the laundry-man did. He's a new man, too – he just *might* have taken Scamper.'

The grocer was very concerned to hear about Scamper. He called to the back of the shop. 'Reggie – come here a minute. You delivered goods at the farm today, didn't you?'

A big burly man came out, red-faced and smiling. 'Yes – I did. Anything wrong?'

'This boy's dog has gone and they're afraid he's been stolen. He'd like to know if you saw the dog anywhere around when you delivered the groceries.'

'What sort of a dog?'

'A golden spaniel,' said Peter at once.

'No. I didn't see any dog at the farm,' said

the man. 'Though I do recollect seeing him once or twice. Very friendly, he was.'

'Well – thanks,' said Peter's father, and walked out of the shop.

'He *might* have taken Scamper,' said Peter. 'He's the kind of man that would make heavy footprints in the snow, Dad. He's heavy and tall and has big feet.'

'That's true,' agreed his father. 'I took a look at his great feet, too. But he has such an open, honest face, Peter. And I took a look at the grocer's van, too – it was standing outside the shop. Did you notice?'

'No,' said Peter. 'Why – was there anything peculiar about it?'

'It was quite an ordinary van,' said his father, 'but it only had a roof – it was open at both ends so that goods could be easily put in and out, and . . .'

'And that means that Scamper *couldn't* have been taken away in it – he'd have jumped out – or at any rate been seen,' said Peter. 'Yes, Dad – you're right. We'll have to rule out the grocer's man. That's two people in the clear.'

'That leaves the boys who were collecting for

something, the postman, and old Mrs Hughes who comes for the mending,' said his father. 'Well, I *really* think we can say the small boys had nothing to do with the matter . . .'

'I don't see why!' said Peter. 'Scamper likes children. He might quite well have gone off with them for a walk. He wouldn't go with a grown-up – but he does like children.'

'Well, look – there's one of the boys!' said his father. 'See, over there. And he has a dog with him – a terrier. Let's ask him if he saw Scamper this morning. Hey, Alfred – come here a minute. You question him, Peter. He might be scared of me.'

Alfred came over, rather shyly, his dog on a lead beside him, wagging its tail eagerly.

'Alfred – you came to the farm this morning, didn't you – with John, your brother,' said Peter. 'Did you see our dog Scamper there?'

'Yes,' said the boy. 'He came up and wagged his tail at my dog Buster here, and they rubbed noses like anything. And we got fifty pence each for our collecting-box. We collect for Sick Animals – we're very fond of animals. We've collected over fifteen pounds now. Scamper wanted to come with us, he seemed to like Buster. I hope your dog isn't lost.'

'I hope not too,' said Peter, with a sigh. 'What time did you come to the house?'

'About half-past eleven, I think – maybe a bit later,' said Alfred.

'Thanks very much,' said Peter. 'Well, Dad, we can rule out anyone who came before a quarter to twelve, because Scamper was about then, when those boys came. It must be someone who came between then and the time we left the meeting. That narrows it down a bit.'

'We'll go back and have some lunch,' said his father. 'We can't do much more now. If ONLY Scamper would come rushing up to meet us!'

CHAPTER THIRTEEN

A meeting about Scamper

NOBODY WANTED much dinner that day, even though it was more than half an hour late! 'I can't seem to *swallow* properly,' complained Janet. 'Mother, *where* do you think Scamper is? Do you think he could have gone up to the hills to see Matt?'

'Well, no, darling,' said Mother. 'He doesn't usually rush all the way up the hills to see Matt, especially when snow is on the ground.'

'Well, we've seen one of the boys who came here this morning – and we've seen the grocer's man, and though he's big and hefty and wears large boots, *he's* not the thief. He has an open van, so if he had taken Scamper, Scamper would have jumped out or made an awful noise.'

'And we can rule out the laundry-man because he came at a quarter-past eleven and didn't see Scamper. Did you let him out of the shed by any chance?' said Mother.

'We did,' said Janet. 'He scratched at the door, so out he went!'

'That leaves the postman, and old Mrs Hughes who came to collect the mending,' said Mother. '*Neither* of them could have taken Scamper. Mrs Hughes is absolutely terrified of dogs, and if the postman took away Scamper, everybody would have seen Scamper walking beside him, back to the post-office. I do feel it must be someone like the man who came asking for farm-work.'

'Well, I saw that fellow myself, and he didn't in the *least* fit the description the police give of the dog-thief,' said Dad. 'He was a skinny little fellow, small and underfed, with feet like a woman. He looked as if he'd run for his life if a dog so much as sniffed at him.'

'That only leaves Mrs Hughes,' said Peter.

'Well, you must know quite certainly that *that* poor old thing wouldn't steal a penny, let alone a dog,' said Mother. 'She loves Scamper, and always brings him a titbit when she calls for the mending.'

'A titbit!' said Janet. 'Oh, Mother – do you think this morning's titbit had a sleeping-pill in it? Do you think Scamper ate the titbit and fell asleep, and Mrs Hughes . . .'

'Now *do* you imagine that that poor little old lady could *possibly* carry a heavy dog like Scamper all the way from here to the village?' said her mother. 'This is getting ridiculous. For goodness' sake, eat your lunch and be sensible. If you're going to go about suspecting innocent people, I shall be very cross.'

'Let's have another meeting and talk about the whole thing,' said Peter, seeing that Janet was near tears at being spoken to so sharply. 'If six of us talk round and round the matter, we may think of something.'

'I don't want a meeting without Scamper,' said Janet, beginning to cry. 'It's horrid not knowing who's taken him. It doesn't seem to be ANYONE who came here today, so who can it be?'

'I've a good mind to go all round the village and look for men with very large feet,' said

Peter, banging the table and making everyone jump.

'Oh, don't be silly,' said his mother. 'You can't possibly go up to anyone with large feet and say "Please, have you stolen my dog? Your feet are big, so you may have done so."'

Peter just couldn't help smiling at this, though the smile disappeared almost at once. 'All right, Mother, I think I'll call a meeting and see what the others have to say. Have you finished, Janet? Hurry up, then. I'll go and see George, and we'll collect the others.'

It was a relief to have something to do. Waiting about, hoping against hope to see the beloved golden figure come padding up, tail waving, was very upsetting. Peter went off to George's house.

'Dear old Scamper's been stolen,' he told the startled George. 'I'm calling a meeting again, at once. Please don't start sympathising with me too much, George, else I shall howl. Will you go round and tell the others?'

'Of course!' said George, shocked. He patted Peter on the back. 'Cheer up. The Secret Six will get him back!' Off he went, and soon he had rounded up the rest of the club – Colin, Pam and Barbara. They were horrified at the news.

'There now!' said Pam. 'I was *afraid* of Scamper being stolen as soon as I heard the news that my granny's Snowy had gone. Let's get to the meeting shed, quick!'

On the way there, they met Susie, Binkie, Bony and Jack. 'Ha!' called Susie at once. 'Going to have a meeting of the Secret Six? Have you turned anyone else out yet? I'm expecting any minute to hear you're the Secret Two!'

'Shut up,' said Pam, rudely. 'We're going to have a most important meeting – about Scamper. He's been stolen.'

'Oh, I expect he's just run away,' said Susie. 'I would too, if I were Peter's dog.'

'SUSIE! Be quiet,' said an angry voice. It was Jack's. He called to George. 'George – is that true? Has old Scamper really been stolen?'

'Well – we're not absolutely sure,' said George, cautiously, not certain if Peter would approve of him giving information to Jack, now that he wasn't a member. 'Anyway, it can't be of any interest to you now.'

The French boy hadn't understood properly. He turned to Jack. 'He say something of a dog – what dog?'

'*Le petit chien s'en va!*' said Susie, very pleased with herself. '*Il est* – er – *stolen!*'

'*Mais, ça, c'est terrible*,' said Bony, and Jack couldn't help nodding. It *was* terrible to hear that Scamper had been stolen. Whatever would Janet and Peter do without him? Jack wished and wished he still belonged to the Secret Seven – how eagerly he would have helped to try and find dear old Scamper!

'Serves Peter right!' said Susie, and was amazed to receive a really hard shove from Jack. He glared at his sister. 'If you say that again, I'll – I'll push you into the pond!' he said. And dear me – he really *meant* it! Susie didn't dare to say one more word!

CHAPTER FOURTEEN

Something to do

EVERYONE ARRIVED promptly for the meeting. They came to the shed in a bunch, and knocked. The password was said, and in they all went. For once in a way, Peter didn't even look to see if everyone was wearing the S. S. badge!

'You all know that – that – the meeting's about – about poor old Scamper,' he said, giving a little choke. Pam reached out and patted his arm, tears in her eyes.

'We're terribly, awfully sorry, Peter,' she said. 'But we'll find him – we *will*. We've never failed in anything yet.'

Peter gave them a quick outline of the people who had come to the house that morning, both before and after Scamper had left the meeting.

'We ought to question every single one of them,' said George, sternly.

'Well, most of them *have* been questioned,' said Peter. 'Especially the two with vans – they could so easily have popped Scamper into a van. But we know they didn't. And the man who came after a job is in the clear, too – he was very small, my father said – and we do know that the dog-thief has large feet and must be a big man.'

'And it's not the two little boys,' said Janet. 'Anyway, they came to collect for Sick Animals, so they'd hardly steal a dog.'

'And it's not old Mrs Hughes – she's afraid of dogs,' said Peter. 'Anyway, she's an old darling. And then there's Postie, the postman. You all know *him* – he's a tiny fellow, always bright and cheery. I should think his boots are no bigger than Janet's.'

'Well, someone would have seen him with Scamper, if he *had* taken him,' said Colin. 'He has to go from house to house and heaps of people would have seen Scamper walking with him – and I just can't imagine that he *carried*

Scamper – as the thief would have to do, with a dog fast asleep from drugged meat.'

'Well, if that's all the people who came to the house, and not one of them took Scamper, he MUST be somewhere around,' said Pam. 'Maybe he's hurt himself – maybe he's lying somewhere about, waiting for you to go to his help.'

'Pam – *can* you imagine Scamper lying somewhere without giving a single bark, or howl or whine?' said Peter, impatiently. 'Do be sensible. Now – has anyone any suggestions?'

Nobody had! They sat and looked at each other, trying their hardest to think of some good idea.

'Well?' said Peter, looking from one to the other. Colin was the only one to answer.

'I'm going to do the only possible thing,' he said. 'Something already suggested at our last meeting. I'm simply going to keep my eyes open for a heavy man with rather large feet – and follow him home. If he's the one who's taken Scamper, he'll probably have him there – and if I yell out "Scamper!" at the top of my

voice, he's sure to bark – even if he can't come running out, because of being tied up.'

'It does seem to be about the only thing we can do,' said George, frowning. 'Though I've no doubt that the village will be *crowded* with big men and large feet! Well, I'm going to start this very afternoon. The sooner the better. Shall we close this meeting, Peter, and get on with the job? It will be dark pretty early today.'

'Right,' said Peter. 'But for goodness' sake don't get into trouble, any of you – I mean, don't let anyone you're following *guess* that you're tracking them.'

'Of course we won't,' said Pam. 'I'm glad we've something to *do*. It's no use setting about moping – thought I feel I could quite well howl when I begin to think about what might have happened to dear old Scamper. Oh, I *wish* he'd come scratching at the door, I *wish* he'd . . .'

'Shut up, Pam,' said George, seeing that Janet was beginning to look upset. 'Well, Peter – shall we go? When shall we report anything – *if* we have anything to report?'

'Oh, *immediately*,' said Peter. 'Either Janet or I will be at the house. Gosh – I hope someone *does* have something to report. Well, goodbye, all of you. See you again soon.'

They trooped out of the shed, and Peter shut the door carefully and locked it, putting the key under the stone as usual. He and Janet went back to the house.

'I don't feel very hopeful, do you, Janet?' said Peter miserably. 'We can't really expect to

do better than Dad, or the police.'

'Well – with seven of us – oh dear, I mean *six*, of course – watching out – there's just a chance we may hit on something,' said Janet. 'I just do wish I could stop myself from expecting to see Scamper come rushing round the corner.

I wonder what the others will do this afternoon in their search for large-footed men. I know *one* man who has the biggest feet *I* ever saw.'

'Who?' said Peter, at once. 'Quick – *who*? He might be the thief.'

'Well, he's not. He's the tall policeman that came to see Daddy!' said Janet.

The other four had walked down into the town together, talking. They split up at the station, and went their different ways. Colin said he was not going home – he was going to sit down on the seat outside the station, and watch different people go by. 'I *may* see someone who's just the type we want,' he said. 'Goodbye – and good luck! Keep your eyes open – if that thief *is* here in this village, we're bound to see him sooner or later.'

Colin sat on the seat for a minute or two, watching the passers-by – and then he sat up straight. A man walked by with a heavy step – a man with outsize shoes – a burly man with a not very pleasant face. '*And* he's carrying a dog!' said Colin, in the greatest excitement. 'I'll follow him. I'LL FOLLOW HIM!'

CHAPTER FIFTEEN

Colin does a little trailing

THE LARGE-FOOTED man walked heavily down the street, still carrying the dog. It wriggled a little and the man put it down. It whined and dragged back, trying to get off the lead.

Colin couldn't help feeling excited. 'The dog is trying to escape,' he thought. 'And what a

beauty it is – a tiny miniature poodle – must be worth a lot of money. Has he stolen it? It seems a bit rash to carry it through the town, if so, but he may have stolen it from miles away. Nobody here would recognise it, then.'

He kept as close to the man as he could. The fellow did not walk fast, but took such enormous strides that Colin had to hurry to keep behind him. The man came to the bus-stop and sat down there, on the seat for waiting passengers. Colin debated what to do. Perhaps he had better sit down too. So down he sat. The little dog whined and strained towards the boy, and the man pulled him roughly back.

'Shame!' thought Colin. 'Dragging him away from me so unkindly. I'm sure he doesn't belong to the man. People aren't rough with their own little dogs. I shall certainly go on watching him.'

After about five minutes the man got up and went on again. Colin leapt up too, and followed. The man was now carrying the dog under his arm – and then suddenly, to Colin's great surprise, he tucked the little thing right inside his coat, so that it couldn't be seen!

'Now why?' thought the boy, puzzled. 'Goodness – there's a policeman coming along – the man didn't want him to see the dog, I suppose. This is VERY, VERY suspicious! I must certainly keep on his trail.'

The man took Colin for rather a long walk – up a steep hill, down the other side, and then round and back to the town again. He put the little dog down once, for a trot, and then popped him under his arm once more.

At last he came to the gate of a small house. He set the dog down, and it at once ran up to the front door. Colin stopped near the gate and watched.

The man stood there at the gate, holding it open. He spoke to Colin.

'Do come in! You've been following me about for miles, goodness knows why. Is there anything interesting about me? Or are you practising trailing for the Scouts, or something? Pray come in! You're quite a good trailer, if rather conspicuous. And if you don't know what that word means, let me tell you that it means "easily seen". I've had my eye on you all the way, young man, though you thought I hadn't spotted you. You don't by any chance want to steal this little miniature poodle, do you?'

Colin simply didn't know *what* to say. He stood there, gaping. The man pushed him through the gate and up to the front door, holding him quite firmly by the arm.

An old lady stood at the door. She had just opened it, and at once saw the tiny poodle. She picked it up and fondled it.

'Diddums enjoy his walkie-walk then?' she said, and kissed the poodle on the top of his head. 'Who's this boy, John?'

'I've no idea,' said the man, and pushed Colin in front of him. 'He has followed me very carefully for miles. Maybe he wanted to steal Diddums!'

'Oh, the wicked boy! Surely he's not that dreadful dog-thief who's been going about,' cried the old lady, and she hugged the tiny poodle to her. 'Let's call the police.'

'Oh, no – please don't!' said Colin, in great alarm. 'I'm not a dog-thief, honestly I'm not. I – I thought perhaps *you* might be. It – well – you see – well, it's not often you see a *man* carrying a tiny poodle – I mean, they're really lap-dogs – dogs for women, aren't they? I – I . . .'

By this time he had been pushed into the house, and the front door was shut. Colin felt more and more alarmed.

'Please don't call the police, please let me go. My father would be awfully angry with me. You see, my friend has had his golden spaniel stolen, and we're trying to find it for him. We're all of us looking out for a large-footed man, and . . .'

'And I've large feet – and was carrying a valuable dog. Well, you certainly puzzled me this afternoon. I hope you enjoyed your walk?'

'May I go please?' said Colin, desperately. 'I apologise, I do really. I expect we'll make a lot of mistakes before we catch the thief.'

'I rather think you will,' said the man. 'No, I shan't let you go yet. Don't look so alarmed. I was just about to ask you to share a bottle of ginger-beer with me – with a slice or two of lemon in it. Very nice that way. Mother, will you get us some – and a few buns as well?'

Colin heaved an enormous sigh of relief.

This man wasn't *really* angry, after all, and now that he could look closely at him, he saw that he had a merry twinkle in his eye. Thank goodness! Colin decided that he would be much more careful about trailing anyone in future. To think that the man had known he was behind him all the time!

He enjoyed the ginger-beer and buns, said thank you very politely, and escaped, the tiny dog following him to the door.

'Gosh!' said Colin, scurrying home. 'I've done *my* bit today. I wonder how the others are getting on!'

Well, let's find out! Pam and Barbara are off on their own – what luck have *they* had?

CHAPTER SIXTEEN

Jack puzzles his brains

PAM AND Barbara had decided to work together in their task of trying to find the dog-thief.

'Two heads are better than one!' said Pam, and off they went. 'Now to look for tall, burly men with big feet.'

But alas – the tall, burly men they saw had small feet – and the only men with large feet were *little* fellows! The girls were rather surprised.

'It seems the wrong way round,' said Pam, examining the feet of an enormous coalman heaving a sack of coal over his shoulder. 'Look how tiny this man's feet are! He *ought* to wear shoes size 12 at least! He's SO BIG!'

'Anything wrong with my feet, miss?' said

the coalman, astonished to have them stared at so closely. The two girls went red, muttered something and ran off. They hardly dared to examine anyone's feet after that!

They saw Colin in the distance, and decided to walk in the opposite direction.

'No good *all* of us meeting and looking at the same people,' said Pam sensibly, and turned up a long, very quiet road that seemed to go on for miles. It ended in a lane that ran between fields. In a nearby field stood a large old rambling house, with many sheds, big and little, round it. The girls walked on down the lane – and then Pam suddenly caught hold of Barbara's arm, making her jump.

'Barbara – can you hear that noise?'

'What noise? Oh – that's only dogs barking,' said Barbara.

'*Only* dogs barking! Aren't we *looking* for dogs? Well, do you see that lonely old house with all those sheds around, set in the fields? Wouldn't that be a marvellous place to keep stolen dogs? I *bet* Scamper's there – *and* Matt's collie – *and* Snowy, my granny's dog!'

'Oh, Pam – no – why *should* they be there?' said Barbara. 'It's probably just ordinary dog-kennels – you know, kennels kept by someone who takes care of people's dogs when they go away.'

'Well, I'm going to LOOK!' said Pam. 'And what is more, I'm going to stand outside that high fence round the place, and yell "SNOWY! SCAMPER! and SHADOW!"'

'Oh – well, that's not a bad idea,' said Barbara, feeling suddenly excited. Supposing all the stolen dogs *were* there – what a thrill it would be! What heroines she and Pam would be, too!

The two girls went boldly up to the fence. Pam asked Barbara to hoist her up, so that she could see over the top. Up she went, and gazed on a mass of small and big sheds, each with their own little yards. Dogs of all kinds and shapes were there, barking, whining, running about . . .

Pam began to shout at the top of her voice. 'SCAMPER! SHADOW! SNOWY! SCAMPER, SCAMPER!'

The dogs heard the shouts and fell silent, all of them staring across the yards at the shouting girl. Then they began to answer back – WHAT a row they made! Some were excited, some were angry, some just wanted to make a noise.

A young woman and a man came running out of the house to see what was the matter. They quietened the dogs in a trice, and then saw Pam, up on the fence. The man said something to a dog by his side, and it raced out of the front gate and round the fence to the two girls, growling. Pam and Barbara were absolutely terrified. They both sat on the top of the fence, yelling for help!

The man and the girl came up, looking very angry. 'What do you think you're doing, shouting at my dogs like that?' he said. 'You be careful they don't get loose and attack you.'

'Please call off this fierce dog below us,' said Pam, beginning to cry with fright. 'We – we were only calling out the names of some stolen dogs we know, to see if any of them were here.'

'You little idiots!' said the man. 'We're dog *breeders*, not dog-thieves! Bob, leave the girls alone – down, Bob. Now you go, you two, and don't yell at our dogs

again. Bob won't hurt you – he'll just see you off the field.'

Very timidly the two girls jumped down from the fence and walked past the dog Bob, and out of the field. Bob watched them sharply all the way, as if he meant to see that they didn't help themselves even to a snowball! They were most relieved to be safely back on the road again.

'I think that was rather silly of us,' said Barbara. 'Don't let's do anything like that again. Let's go to the dairy and buy ice-creams. I feel I need something like that.'

They crossed the road to go to the dairy, and Pam suddenly nudged Barbara's arm.

'Look – there's Jack, all by himself. Shall we speak to him? That awful Susie isn't with him, nor Bony or Skinny, or whatever that French boy's name is.'

Jack had seen the two girls, but turned away. Pam called to him.

'Jack! Come and have an ice-cream!'

Jack looked surprised and pleased, but shook his head. 'No thanks – it's awfully kind of you – but – well, I'm busy.'

'We've been looking for the dog-thief,' said Barbara. 'But we've had no luck. Are *you* looking for him too – even though you're not in the club now?'

'I might be,' said Jack, cautiously. 'Well – I can't stop now. As I said – I'm busy.'

Yes – Jack *was* busy. He didn't belong to the Secret Seven – or Six – any more, but that wasn't going to stop him from looking for dear old Scamper! He had met Colin, who had told him everything he knew – told him all about the visitors to the farm that morning – the laundry-man, Mrs Hughes, the two boys, the postman, the man asking for work, the grocer's man . . . 'And not one single one of them could have stolen Scamper,' said Colin. 'Not one! The police just don't know *who* took Scamper – but they're pretty certain it's the same thief who took the other dogs, and left his enormous footprints in the snow, when he stole the dogs at night.'

And now Jack was busy on his own. What was he doing? What had he found out? How the two girls would have loved to know!

Jack had been thinking very hard since he

had heard the whole story from Colin of Scamper's disappearance. The dog certainly had been stolen – there was no doubt about that – but WHY hadn't he barked or howled when he was taken away? That was what puzzled Jack. And why hadn't the *other* stolen dogs made a fuss too?

'The police thought that the dogs didn't make a noise because they had eaten some drugged meat, or something like that thrown down by the thief – and had fallen asleep, and then had been carried away,' thought Jack. 'But the thief must surely always have had a car or a van or lorry to pop the dog into? After all, how *could* a big dog like Matt's collie have been carried off – unless in some kind of car or van? I know the thief is supposed to be big and burly – but even so, people would notice *any* man carrying a large, sleeping dog.'

He sat on his bed and puzzled his brains for a long time. Susie banged at his door, but he wouldn't answer. Somehow, somewhere, there must be a clue that would fit this odd problem – some key to unlock the mystery.

'ALL the dogs must have known the thief, or

they certainly wouldn't have eaten any food he threw down,' said Jack to himself. 'Scamper wouldn't dream of touching any food given to him by a stranger – and he definitely wouldn't go off with anyone he didn't know. He'd bark the place down! So the thief *must* have been someone that all the dogs knew – someone that every one of them trusted and liked very much – just as they love Bony and will follow him anywhere. Bother – who *is* this peculiar thief, loved and trusted by dogs everywhere? It *must* be one of those seven people who went to the farm this morning.'

He decided to go out for a walk – but that sister of his would want to go with him, and take Bony as well! Jack was getting very tired of Bony. He went to the window and looked out – no one was in the garden. He slid down the pear-tree outside and was out in the road before anyone had spotted him.

'I shall think better when I'm walking,' thought Jack, hopefully. 'Hallo, there's old Mrs Hughes. *She* was one of the visitors at the farm this morning.'

Before he could go over and say 'Hallo' a

small dog came bounding up to the old lady. She gave a horrified shriek and tried to beat it off with her stick. Jack went to the rescue at once.

'Well!' he thought, as the dog ran off down the road, tail between its legs. 'Well – it certainly was NOT Mrs Hughes who took Scamper away. I'd better take the old lady home – she's really scared!'

It was on the way to Mrs Hughes's house that Jack saw Postie, the smiling little postman, delivering letters.

'Oh, postman, I've been so scared by a little black dog,' said the old lady in her quavering voice, and Postie nodded.

'Ay, ma'am – I

know how scared you are of dogs. Anyone that's been bitten once IS frightened of them. I've never been bitten, and it's a good thing I'm not scared of them, for I meet so many when I'm out delivering letters.'

'Ah, but they love you, don't they, Postie?' said the old lady. 'You're kind to them. I've seen them run up to you in the street, tails a-wagging. How I wish *you'd* find that dog-thief for us.'

'I wish I could, madam,' said Postie. 'He must be a cruel, hard-hearted fellow, that.' He went through a nearby gate to deliver a letter and at once a dog came bounding to welcome him, licking in delight.

'Well, little Tim the terrier, how are you?' said Postie, and patted the excited dog, who followed him right to the house and back to the gate. Jack watched. If anyone could persuade a dog to go with him, the postman could! But he was not in the *least* like the thief. He should be tall, burly and have large feet – and he should surely have a car or a van to take away a dog.

'Now suppose Postie threw down a bit of drugged meat to *that* dog – and he ate it and fell asleep – Postie couldn't POSSIBLY carry him off over his shoulder without being seen. Everybody he met would notice the dog he was carrying, and ask him questions. I wonder if the *grocer's* man is loved by dogs – *he* had a van. No – he's been ruled out, Colin said. Well, this is a real puzzle!'

Jack suddenly decided to follow the postman, and see if all the dogs at the houses he went to made a fuss of him. So he trailed Postie, carefully keeping out of sight. Yes – every single dog belonging to any house the postman went to, welcomed him with the utmost delight.

'*Just* as if he were old Bony,' thought Jack. 'What on earth is there about Bony and Postie that makes dogs adore them? It beats me! A sort of gift, I suppose.'

He trailed the postman back to the post office, and was just about to go home, when Postie came out again. He had no post-bag this time, and he grinned at Jack.

'Hallo!' he said. 'I'm off home now. Done at last. I've walked miles today! My poor feet are tired out!'

Jack didn't know where the postman lived, but he decided to see. Did he have a dog of his own? Probably he had two or three. He trailed Postie carefully, keeping out of sight, and saw him go into a small cottage not far away. A plump little woman was in the garden, taking in some washing. She was so like the postman that Jack guessed she was his sister.

'Hallo, Tommy,' she called. 'Your meal's in the kitchen, and the teapot's on the hob. Help yourself! Are you going out again tonight? There's more snow forecast.'

'Yes, Liz. I've got to go out,' said Postie. 'Another delivery, you know. It'll be nice and dark then.'

Jack frowned. '*Nice* and dark.' Why '*Nice* and dark'? Why should the postman be glad of the dark? Jack shook himself. 'Don't be silly!' he thought. 'You CAN'T suspect the postman! He LOVES dogs – and they love him!'

CHAPTER SEVENTEEN

Jack makes a surprising discovery

NEXT MORNING everyone in the town was talking about the same thing.

'ANOTHER dog has been stolen! Have you heard? It's Mr Kaye's beautiful little prize pup – his Alsatian. Only four months old, and worth a large sum of money. Goodness knows what he paid for it.'

It was Mrs Cook at the farm who told Peter and Janet. 'Heard the latest news?' she said. 'That dog-thief has been at work again. Mr Kaye's Alsatian pup has been stolen.'

'Who told you?' said Janet.

'Postie,' said Mrs Cook. 'He was that upset. 'Another lovely dog gone!' he said. And he inquired after old Scamper, hoping he had come back. This is a terrible business, isn't it? No dog is safe, it seems to me. And it's always the valuable ones that go.'

Jack, too, heard the news, and frowned. Yet another dog! A fairly big one too, although only a pup. He knew Mr Kaye and decided to go and see him.

He arrived on Mr Kaye's doorstep just as he was saying goodbye to two policemen, who had come to get particulars of the theft.

'Well, we'll do what we can, sir,' said one of the men, 'but not one of the stolen dogs have we found yet – nor even heard of. It's a very clever thief that's at work, sir – but we'll get him – don't you worry yourself, sir.'

'I'm worried about my *dog*,' said Mr Kaye. 'I was very fond of him. That thief deserves to – to . . .' And then he saw Jack, and stopped. 'What do you want, Jack?' he said. 'Heard about my poor pup?'

'Yes,' said Jack. 'I came to say I'm very sorry. Is there anything I can do for you?'

'Well, that's nice of you,' said Mr Kaye. 'Come in. I'll tell you about Sasha – that's the pup. It's a mystery to me how he was stolen – a mystery. He wouldn't go anywhere with anyone, except me – and he was getting a big dog, you know – I mean, if anyone tried to take him by force, he'd fly at them.'

He took Jack into his sitting-room, and showed him a photograph of Sasha.

'Lovely, isn't he?' he said. 'I'm offering a

large reward for him. I paid over two hundred pounds for that pup, you know.'

'When did he disappear?' asked Jack.

'Last night – about half-past six,' said Mr Kaye. 'It was pitch-dark, and had been snowing. I let Sasha out for a bit, in the front garden – but when I called him, he didn't come. I hunted and hunted for him, took my torch out – and all I found were Sasha's paw-marks – and some very large footprints in the snow in my front garden. The police tell me it's been just the same with the other stolen dogs – some large-footed fellow comes along when a dog is let out for a short run – and the dog is never heard of again. Not a bark or a growl did I hear.'

'Anyone call on you yesterday evening?' asked Jack.

'Not that I know of,' said Mr Kaye. 'No – I don't remember asking anyone in last night. We were very quiet, my wife and I. It's nice of you to take such an interest, my boy, very nice.'

'Well, I do hope Sasha will turn up again,' said Jack. 'You're *sure* nobody called?'

'I'd remember if I'd had any visitors, my boy

– so would my wife – and we'd be *most* suspicious of them,' said Mr Kaye. 'Well, goodbye – and many thanks.'

Jack went down the drive to the front gate, frowning. He saw all kinds of footprints, both large and small – no good hoping to learn anything from those. A great many people seemed to have been walking all over the snowy garden, and the thief's footprints would be well and truly spoilt – all mixed up with everyone else's.

'This is a real puzzle that seems to have no solution,' thought Jack. 'Look at the way the thief took Scamper – no one saw him – no one heard him – and he wasn't any of the people who were known to come to the house. Who *was* he, and how did he manage to creep up to the farmhouse, watch for Scamper – and *get him*! And then take him away without a single person seeing him! It absolutely *beats* me! And yet there must be a simple answer to it all – an answer that even the police can't see! And WHERE are the dogs taken to? They simply disappear off the face of the earth, it seems. But they must be *somewhere* because obviously the thief only steals them because they are worth selling.'

Jack's thoughts came back to what he had heard the postman say – 'It'll be nice and dark then.' '*Nice and dark*' – why did the postman and his sister think that darkness was desirable? Could he *possibly* be in league with the thieves? After all, it was soon after he had said the night was 'nice and dark' that Sasha, Mr Kaye's Alsatian pup had been stolen.

'It obviously can't be the postman who is the thief,' thought Jack. 'He's little, not big – his feet are small and wouldn't make large prints in the snow – he adores dogs, and presumably wouldn't wish to steal them from their comfortable homes – and he couldn't POSSIBLY have taken away Scamper, because, if he had, someone would have seen Scamper running beside him. All the same – I think I'll go to Postie's house this afternoon, and have a little snoop round. I suppose he *might* have a cellar to hide dogs in. No – I'm getting silly. That tiny cottage *couldn't* have a cellar.'

He set off to the cottage about four o'clock that afternoon. Nobody was there. The front door and back door were both locked. Postie was obviously out on his rounds – Liz, his sister, was probably shopping. It really would be a good chance to poke round a bit.

'Not that I expect to find anything that will help,' said Jack to himself. 'I'm probably on a real wild-goose chase. I hope Postie or his sister don't come back and catch me. I'd get into real trouble then.'

He looked all round the little garden. He tried the handle of the garden shed, but it was locked. He peeped in at the kitchen window. He felt extremely guilty all the time and half-ashamed of himself. Whatever would his father say if he saw him? Then he remembered old Matt the shepherd and his sorrow for his lost collie – and thought of Peter and Janet, and their tears for Scamper.

'It's no good – I just *must* discover all I can that might be of help,' he thought.

He went back to the little shed, and peered through the small, dirty window, switching on his torch. It was difficult to see anything clearly at first, but after a while his eyes grew used to the shadows inside the shed, and he could make

out some flower-pots, an old broom – and something else – something rather surprising! Yes, VERY surprising!

Jack stared and stared – and then suddenly heard a noise that made him stop staring and rush to climb over the fence at the end of the garden, and get away. A car had just driven up to the cottage gate – Jack heard the engine purr, and then stop. He caught a glimpse of it, in the light of a nearby lamp-post – a red van – gosh, it was the post-office van, that delivered parcels – Postie must have come back home to have a cup of tea! Jack fled away over the field at the back of Postie's garden, and disappeared. What a narrow escape! Another few seconds, and he would have been caught! Whew!

CHAPTER EIGHTEEN

Well done, Jack

JACK RACED home at top speed, his mind in a whirl. He couldn't forget what he had seen in that shed. He must tell someone, he must. If what he had seen meant what he thought it did, the great Dog Mystery was solved!

He bumped into Susie and Bony at the gate, and Susie caught hold of him.

'What's the matter? Why do you look so excited? You've *got* to tell me!'

Jack shook himself free. Goodness, he certainly couldn't cope with Susie just now. He'd better go up to the farm – yes, he *must* see Peter and Janet, even though he no longer belonged to the Secret Seven.

So, to Susie's anger and amazement, he shot

off down the road, and then raced up to the farm, panting for all he was worth. He hammered on the front door.

'Good gracious – it's you, Jack – whatever's the matter?' said Peter, opening the door.

'Peter – it's important,' gasped Jack. 'I believe I know who the dog-thief is. Where's your father?'

'In the study,' said Peter, his eyes nearly falling out of his head. 'Quick – this way.'

Soon Jack was standing in the study, with a most surprised family listening to him.

'I think I know who stole Scamper!' he said. 'In fact, I'm CERTAIN!'

'Who?' said the children's father, sharply.

'The *postman* – old Postie!' said Jack. There was an amazed silence, and then Peter spoke.

'Impossible!' he said. 'Isn't it, Dad? The police say that the man had very large feet, and made big, deep footprints – and he probably had a van to take away the dogs.'

'The postman is very small with tiny feet,' said Mother.

'Well, I'll tell you what I saw in his shed a little while ago,' said Jack. 'I saw a HUGE pair of boots – really enormous! Now what would Postie want with *those*? They certainly weren't the right size for *his* small feet – so it's my guess that he wore them when he went out in the snow to steal Snowy – and to steal Shadow, up on the snowy hills. In fact, to steal *any* dog on a snowy night – leaving huge footprints behind to mislead everyone. I bet if you got hold of those boots, and looked at the copies of the footprints that the police have, they'd match EXACTLY!'

'But what about *Scamper*?' said Peter. 'Scamper wasn't stolen in the snow – he just disappeared. We *know* he didn't go with Postie, or he'd have been seen walking down to the village with him.'

'Did Postie bring any parcels for you yesterday?' asked Jack, and saw Mother nod her head. 'Right! Then he must have used the parcels *delivery* van – he could easily have patted Scamper's head, and made him follow him to the van – pushed him in, slammed the door – and driven off with him. Nobody would know. Scamper loved him, so he probably wouldn't even have barked. I bet he's used that post-office van to shove dogs into plenty of times. I guess he took it up the road that runs alongside the sheep fields the day he left a letter at the hut for old Matt – and took Shadow off with him then. He'd say, "Come along, Shadow," and Shadow would follow him to the van – he'd get a push to send him inside – and slam would go the van door. Easy!'

'This is all very serious,' said the children's father. 'We must be very, very careful that you are right, Jack. Are you quite *sure* that you saw those boots? I didn't think of the post-office van, of course – Postie might quite well have taken Scamper away in it – the dog would follow him anywhere, he knew that Postie was a friend of the family.'

'My guess is that he threw down drugged meat to dogs he wouldn't be able to persuade into the van, waited till they dropped asleep – and then carried them there,' said Jack. 'You know how the police said there were scuffly patches of snow – well, they'd be made when he dragged away the dog.'

'Astounding!' said the children's father. 'Yes, it fits. It all fits. Yes, yes – he'd persuade some dogs to follow him to the van – and shut them in – and the others he would drug – and then drag or carry them to the van. Then off he could go with them – I wonder where?'

'The police will make him say,' said Mother. 'What a wicked fellow he is to cause such trouble and heart-break. Poor old Matt now – he seems to have aged terribly since Shadow was stolen.'

'Mother, he'll look all right again when he gets Shadow back,' cried Janet. 'Oh quick, let's do something. Let's make Postie tell us where he took the dogs. Has he *sold* Scamper? Can we buy him back? Quick, Daddy, quick, Mother.'

'Can't we go and tell the police straight away?' said Peter. '*They* ought to go and make Postie own up, and confess everything, oughtn't they?'

'Yes,' said his father. He turned to Jack and patted him on the back. 'You'll have to come with me, Jack. You've done well – very well. You've succeeded where everyone else has failed. The police will want to know everything you can tell them. Come along.'

'Can we come too?' cried Peter.

'No,' said his father. 'Only Jack. We'll go this very minute. Mother, telephone the police and tell them we're coming, and why.'

He went out into the darkening evening with a beaming Jack. Peter rushed after Jack and caught hold of his arm.

'Oh, Jack! You *are* a marvel! Thank you, thank you for coming with such good news.'

Jack grinned and went off with Peter's father. What an excitement – WHAT an excitement! Good old Jack! Good old everybody!

CHAPTER NINETEEN

All's well again!

PETER AND Janet and their mother could hardly wait for Dad and Jack to return. It seemed AGES before the car could be heard purring up the drive. Janet heard a bark as it drew up, and yelled in delight.

'SCAMPER! It's SCAMPER!' And sure enough it was – dear, silky old Scamper, his ears flopping up and down as he rushed into the hall, his tail wagging nineteen to the dozen. He flung himself on the children, barking loudly in joy. In fact, he couldn't *stop* barking, and was most surprised to find that Janet's face was salty with happy tears, when he licked it.

'And here's SHADOW!' yelled Peter. 'Dad, you've got him too. Is he all right?'

'Perfectly – except that he moped for Matt,' said his father. 'My word, I shall look forward to seeing old Matt's face tomorrow.'

'No, Dad – let him go to Matt tonight,' begged Janet. 'He'll rush up the hills straight as an arrow and find Matt for himself. Matt won't want anyone there when he first sees Shadow again.'

'You're right, Janet darling,' said her mother. 'Put Shadow out of doors, Dad. Let him go to Matt.'

So the door was opened – and the collie shot out like an arrow from a bow! He disappeared into the darkness of the evening, barking wildly.

'He's calling "Matt! Matt! Matt!"' said Janet. 'Oh, Scamper, darling, darling Scamper, I've missed you so. Oh, that horrible Postie – how DARE he steal dogs?'

'What happened when you took the police to Postie's house?' Peter asked Jack.

'Well, nothing very much, really,' said Jack. 'Liz, Postie's sister, was simply terrified when we arrived, and blurted out everything. Postie wasn't there then – he came in later – but by that time Liz had told us that when he went out into the snow at night, he *did* wear those enormous boots I saw, to make people think that the dog-thief was a great big man. He stamped his feet hard into the ground, to make deep prints, as if he were very heavy.'

'Most of the dogs came to him willingly, according to Liz,' said his father. 'Others he drugged as we thought, by giving them meat with pills in. The odd thing is that *every* dog adores him – he had no trouble at all.'

'Where did he take them?' asked Mother.

'To a friend of his, four miles away, who is a vet – it's his second cousin, I believe. And this fellow kept the dogs till all the excitement had died down, and then quietly sold them. Postie must have made a lot of money.'

'Where is Postie now?' asked Janet.

'In a prison-cell,' said her father grimly,

'and he deserves to be well punished. Dog-stealing is a wicked thing – a cruel thing. Thank goodness that Postie's cousin treated the dogs well. Postie used the post-office van to take Scamper away – and many other dogs – and drove them straight to his cousin – so no wonder they seemed to disappear off the face of the earth.'

Mother suddenly put her arms round the smiling, silent Jack, and gave him a hug.

'You shall have a reward,' she said, 'a huge reward – the nicest present you can possibly think of! Clever old Jack! Fancy you snopping round and spotting what those great boots really meant! What shall we give him as a reward, Dad?'

'I don't want ANYTHING!' said Jack, going red. 'My reward is seeing how glad Scamper was to come home! And seeing your faces when he came running indoors!'

Janet went to whisper in Peter's ear, and he nodded eagerly. He turned to Jack.

'Jack – will you do me a favour, please?' he said. 'A very great favour?'

'Of course,' said Jack, at once.

'Then please will you allow me to pin this on to your coat?' said Peter, and pulled out of his pocket the S.S. badge that Jack had refused to take back. 'PLEASE, Jack. We've missed you so. We're all sorry now. We'll have a WONDERFUL meeting tomorrow, down in the shed, and tell everyone your great story – you'll have to tell it yourself – about taking the police out to the shed and everything.'

'All right,' said Jack, his eyes shining as Peter pinned the S.S. badge to his coat. 'I've missed you all too. Now we can be the Secret *Seven* again! Goodness – won't Susie be surprised! I'm longing to see her face! Scamper will be at the meeting too, won't he?'

'Wuff-wuff, wuff-wuff!' said Scamper at once, wagging his tail.

'He says, "Of course, of course!"' said Janet, and she was right!

'And now we'll all have something to eat,' said Mother. 'This kind of thing makes me very hungry. Scamper, let's go and find the largest bone we have.'

Scamper trotted out to the kitchen at once, and soon came back carrying a most enormous bone, and looking very pleased with himself indeed. He took it on the mat to gnaw.

'He hasn't forgotten his manners,' said Mother, pleased. 'I wonder how dear old Shadow is getting on. He must be half-way up the snowy hills by now.'

Yes – Shadow was on his way to Matt, the master he loved. He was bounding over the snow, up the hills to where the sheep were kept. The stars were out now, and their faint light shone down on the long, lean body loping steadily up the hill. If Matt had grieved for Shadow, the collie had certainly grieved for Matt. He had eaten nothing since he had been stolen, and was as lean as a greyhound.

Up he went, and on and on. Ah – there was his master's hut, outlined against the night sky, at the top of the hill. A dim light showed in the tiny window.

Shadow had no breath left to bark, for he had run up the long, long hill without a moment's rest. He came to the hut and hurled himself against the door, panting loudly.

Matt was startled. 'Who's that?' he cried. And then he heard a whine – a whine that made him leap at once from his old wooden chair. Shadow scraped at the bottom of the door, and began to bark. Matt's hands were shaking with joy as he unlocked the door.

'SHADOW, old dog! You've come back to me!' said Matt, in a wondering, trembling voice. Shadow flung himself on the old shepherd, licking him, loving him, whining, his tail waving and wagging without a stop.

Matt sank down on his chair, and Shadow at

once took up his old place, sitting close by the shepherd, his head on his knees, looking up at him with loving brown eyes. Matt put his wrinkled old hand on the dog's soft head.

'I missed you, old friend, I missed you,' he said. 'Like a brother I grieved for you, and my heart was full of sorrow. Where have you come from, this cold night of stars? Did you guess I was waiting for you every hour of the day and night? But I knew you'd come, old dog, I knew you'd come. We'll lie down to sleep in peace tonight – just you and me together.'

Goodbye, old Matt and Shadow; goodbye, Scamper and the Secret Seven. It's good to know you're happy once again!

Look Out, Secret Seven

Contents

CHAPTER ONE

Holidays at last

'HOLIDAYS AT *last*!' said Peter, coming in at the back door, and flinging his school satchel right across the kitchen. It struck the chair that the cat was lying in, and she gave a yowl of fright and disappeared at top speed through the open window.

'Now what did you want to frighten old Puss for?' demanded Rachel, rolling out pastry fiercely. 'Sleeping there peacefully after catching mice all night in your father's barn!'

'I didn't know she was there,' said Peter. 'Honestly I didn't. May I have a dig into that jampot, Rachel?'

'You may not,' said Rachel. 'Where's your sister? Oh my, oh my – holidays again, and you two poking round my kitchen all the time. What a life!'

'Rachel, you'll have *two* people to run your errands, and scrape out dishes, and tell you that your apple-pie is the best in the world,' said Peter. 'And . . .'

'Yes – and two people taking buns out of my tin, and wanting raisins to eat at all times, and asking for homemade lemonade, and . . .'

Janet, Peter's sister, came running in, flung her arms round Rachel and gave her a smacking kiss.

'What's for dinner?' she said.

'You two don't think of anything but food,' grumbled Rachel, giving her pastry a good roll. 'You'd better go into the sitting-room to your mother. Your godmother's with her – and if I know anything about her, she'll have brought you a present – sweets or something.'

Peter and Janet went at once to the sitting-room. They were very fond of their godmother, Auntie Lou. They each gave her a hug, and informed her that the holidays had now begun.

'So we can come over and see you, if you like,' said Peter.

'Wait till you are asked, Peter,' said his mother. 'And what *have* you been doing to your knees? I cannot *think* how you get them so black. Anyone would suppose you walked back from school on them over all the mud you could find.'

'I'll go and wash them,' said Peter, looking down at them in horror. 'Mother, I honestly *don't* know how they . . .'

'Well, just let me give you my little holiday present,' said his godmother. 'I can't wait while you wash your knees, I have to catch the bus. I imagine you still like chocolates?'

And she handed over to him a large tin box, so large that Peter and Janet couldn't believe it contained just chocolates. 'I know you have a club of some sort,' she said. 'Seven or eight of you, aren't there? Well, I thought you'd like this tin of chocolate biscuits for your next meeting.'

Peter took off the lid – and stared in delight.

'Janet, look – dozens and dozens of chocolate biscuits of all kinds! Gosh! Mother, I shall call a meeting at once. Oh, Auntie Lou, you *are* generous! Are they really all for us?'

'For you and your friends,' said his godmother, getting up. 'Now I really must catch my bus. Come and see me off.'

So off they all went to see Auntie Lou safely into the bus. Then back to the sitting-room – and the tin of biscuits.

'Let's not eat a single one ourselves till we call a meeting of the Secret Seven,' said Peter. 'We'll offer them to Mother and Rachel, but we won't take *any* ourselves. It's ages since we had a good meeting – and these will make a meeting go like anything.'

'We'll call one tomorrow,' said Janet, happily. 'Oh, to think it's holidays again – with meetings down in the shed – and passwords and badges, and . . .'

'Passwords – *pass*words – now what in the world was our last one?' said Peter.

'That's easy,' said Janet. 'We chose "Holidays" because we knew the hols would be here when we had the next meeting. I bet everyone remembers it. Let's go round to all the members tonight – or telephone – and tell them there's a meeting tomorrow – at, say, five o'clock.'

'But that's teatime,' said Peter.

'Of course, silly – and those chocolate biscuits will be just right for then,' said Janet.

'Yes – they will,' said Peter. 'Couldn't you write notes to tell the others of the meeting, Janet? It's – well, it's a bit more official.'

'You write them then,' said Janet. 'You're more official than I am. You're the head of the club.'

'Well – perhaps it would be *quicker* to telephone,' said Peter. 'Ha – it will be great to have the Secret Seven going again. I do hope something exciting turns up.'

'It usually does,' said Janet. 'Especially if that awful Susie is about.'

'Jack says Susie's been worse than ever lately,' said Peter. 'If *I* had a sister like Susie I'd sit on her all the time, and . . .'

'Then you'd have a mighty uncomfortable seat!' said Janet. 'Nobody's ever got the better of Susie yet. I bet she'll come to the meeting tomorrow, if she can.'

'Well, she won't get in, if she does come,' said Peter. 'Ah, Scamper – there you are. WHY weren't you here to welcome us back for the holidays?'

Scamper was their lovely golden spaniel. He had been with Matt the shepherd up on the hills, playing with Shadow, Matt's faithful old sheepdog. Then he had suddenly remembered that Peter had told him the holidays began today. HOLIDAYS! Scamper knew that word well – it meant days and days of Peter's and Janet's company, it meant walks, and games, and titbits of all kinds.

So Scamper had given Shadow a sudden apologetic bark, and, to the collie's surprise, had raced down the hill as fast as a hare, his long ears flapping up and down. HOLIDAYS!

Soon he was barking in delight round the two children – and then he suddenly sniffed chocolates. Ha, chocolates – better still!

'You shall have the very first one,' said Janet, taking a biscuit from the top layer. 'Catch!'

Snap! It was in Scamper's mouth – one crunch, and it was gone!

'Biscuits are really *wasted* on you, Scamper,' said Janet. 'I don't believe you even *taste* them. We're calling a meeting of the Secret Seven tomorrow – you'd like to come, wouldn't you?'

'WOOF!' said Scamper, joyfully, his stump of a tail wagging like clockwork. Meetings! Biscuits! Holidays! Woof, woof – life was going to be FUN!

CHAPTER TWO

A shock for the Secret Seven

In the evening Peter and Janet telephoned to the other members of the Secret Seven, and told them about the meeting, and the enormous tin of chocolate biscuits.

'If you'd like to bring something to drink – orangeade or lemonade, for instance, we'll provide the mugs,' said Peter.

Soon all the members knew of the meeting and Peter put down the telephone for the last time. 'Phew – I do hate telephoning,' he said. 'Everyone wants to be so *chatty*!'

'Well, you sounded pretty chatty yourself when you spoke to George and Colin,' said Janet. 'And what a pity Susie came to the telephone when you wanted to speak to Jack!

Now she knows there's a meeting she'll try and play one of her usual silly tricks – I bet she won't give Jack your message.'

'She said she was going to a fancy-dress party tomorrow,' said Peter. 'So we'll be safe from her for once.'

'Oh yes – I remember now,' said Janet. 'Her cousin's giving a fancy-dress affair tomorrow afternoon. I wonder what Susie's going as. That awful friend of hers, Binkie, is going too.'

'Susie said they were going as Jack and Jill,' said Peter. 'But I bet they won't bother to take a pail of water with them. *I'd* like to empty a pail of very, very cold water over Susie's head.'

'You'd never get the chance,' said Janet, with a giggle at the thought of Peter throwing water over that monkey of a Susie. '*She'd* souse *you* before you could stop her.'

'Don't be silly,' said Peter. 'I'd never let her do a thing like that. Now listen – we'll have to be pretty busy tomorrow if we're going to meet in the shed. You'll have to find those green letters, S.S., and pin them on to the door – we took them off because they were getting wet with all that rain, you remember. And for goodness' sake find our badges.'

'I put them away safely in my jewel-case,' said Janet. 'So you needn't worry.'

'Well, I hope you'll find them there,' said Peter. '*Last* time I saw your jewel-case it had sweets in it, and a new rubber, and a bit of sealing-wax, a broken brooch, a . . .'

'You'd no right to look into my jewel-case,' said Janet, 'and I shall . . .'

'All right, all right,' said Peter, hastily. 'Let's not quarrel when there's so much to do. I hope the gardener hasn't taken away the boxes we used to sit on in the shed. And, Scamper, I hope you've been keeping down the mice and rats there for us. I should feel very ashamed of you tomorrow evening if a few rats came to join us.'

'Ugh! What a horrible thought!' said Janet. Scamper gave a loud bark at the same time, as if to tell her that all the rats and mice had been safely dealt with. He decided to go down to the shed the first thing next morning to make quite sure there wasn't even a sniff of them.

It was very pleasant next day to turn out the old shed and make it tidy and clean. The

gardener popped his head in at the door, grunted and went away again, nodding his head in approval of all the tidying up going on.

''Bout time too,' they heard him mutter as he went up the path. Janet looked round the clean shed, pleased with their work. Boxes to sit on – mugs on the little shelf, ready for any drinks that were brought – seven little plastic plates for the biscuits, one for each member – the tin itself standing proudly on a little box of its own – and an old, rather raggedy rug on the earth floor.

'Nice!' said Janet. 'The shed smells a bit of apples, doesn't it, Peter – there were some stored here in the winter, you know. I've put the S.S. on the door. It's a pity the shed has such a small window, it makes it rather dark in here. But it's not dark enough for candles, is it?'

'No,' said Peter. 'Anyway, Mother gets scared if we have candles down here – says Scamper is sure to knock one over and then up would go the shed in flames, and . . .'

'And the fire-engine would come, and we'd have the most exciting meeting we've ever had,' said Janet.

The meeting was to begin at five o'clock, and at five to five Peter, Janet and Scamper were sitting in the shed, waiting. Scamper eyed the tin of biscuits longingly, and gave pathetic little whines, as if to say he was so hungry that he couldn't wait another second for a meal.

Then he suddenly whined excitedly. He had heard footsteps! 'The others are coming,' said Peter, pleased. 'Nice and punctual, too.'

Bang-bang. That was someone knocking on the shed door.

'Password, please!' called Peter, and Pam's and Barbara's voices answered at once.

'Holidays!'

Peter opened the door, grinning. 'Right!' he

said. 'Come in. Hallo, here comes someone else. Password, please!'

'Holidays!' said Colin's voice. No sooner was he in the shed than there came another knock – this time it was George.

'Password!' shouted Peter.

'Peter, is it "Holidays"?' asked George. 'Thank goodness it is! Hey, isn't it nice to be the Secret Seven again? Are we all here? It's a bit dark in the shed this evening.'

'Only Jack to come,' said Peter. 'I think I can hear him now. Yes, here he is. Password, Jack!'

'Holidays', came the answer, and then the door was shut on the Seven. The meeting was about to begin!

And then, very surprisingly, Scamper suddenly began to growl! He sat in a dark corner of the shed and growled and growled without stopping. Everyone stared at him in wonder.

'What's up, Scamper?' asked Peter, but the only answer was another fierce growl. It really was very puzzling.

'Scamper seems to be growling at JACK!' said Pam. 'Look at him staring at him. He's even showing his teeth!'

'He's never done that before to any of us,' said Janet. 'Stop it, Scamper. Jack, take off your cap, perhaps that's why Scamper's growling. You forgot to take it off when you came in.'

'Er – I think I'd better keep it on,' said Jack. 'I've – er – a bit of a cold in my head.'

George suddenly whipped off the cap – and everyone stared in amazement and anger. Hair tumbled, out from under the cap – but not short hair!

'It's SUSIE! Susie, not Jack! Susie, how DARE you dress up in Jack's clothes and come to a meeting?' shouted Peter.

'Well – Binkie and I were on our way home from a fancy-dress party, and we thought we'd

look in on our way past,' grinned Susie. 'We went as Jack and Jill, you see. I'm Jack – and Binkie, who's hiding outside, is Jill. Jack lent me his clothes, so that I could be a boy at the party – and my voice and his are alike, so it was easy to get into your meeting. Ha ha – I heard your password being said – you really are a lot of simpletons, you know – and here I am!'

'And Scamper was the only sensible one among us!' groaned George. '*He* knew it wasn't old Jack sitting here with us! Get out, Susie. GET OUT!'

'With pleasure,' said Susie, and stood up, still with a most infuriating grin on her face. 'Jack will be along here soon. I told him the meeting was at half-past five, instead of five, so it's not his fault he's late. Am I clever enough to be one of the Secret Seven?'

But that was too much for Peter. He gave Susie a push to send her out of the shed, but she wouldn't go, and, instead, began to yell.

'Binkie! Help, Binkie!'

She rushed out of the shed door with all the others following her in a real rage – and then, quite suddenly, something very cold and wet descended on them, soaking their heads and shoulders!

'Oh – sorry – that was the pail of water we took as Jack and Jill!' called Susie, with a squeal of laughter. 'Good shot, Binkie! Good night, all – hope you have a very pleasant meeting!'

And off went the two wicked girls, very pleased indeed with their evening's work. To be One Up on the Secret Seven was wonderful. Oh what a tale to tell their giggling friends!

CHAPTER THREE

A very good meeting

THE SIX left in the shed were too angry for words. Peter shook his fist after the two running girls, and yelled in fury.

'We're soaked! HOW DARE YOU! You wait till we see you again!'

But all the answer they had was the sound of running feet – and distant squeals of laughter. That Susie! How could she even have THOUGHT of such a trick? Poor Jack – fancy having a sister like that!

'Borrowing his clothes too, to be Jack in the nursery rhyme,' groaned Peter, mopping his shoulder with an old sack. 'AND having a pail of water too! I'm wet through!'

'And fancy telling Jack the meeting wasn't

till half-past five – no wonder he's late!' said Janet. 'I'll fetch an old towel from the house, Peter. You're the wettest because you were nearest.'

'No, don't. You'll only have Mother asking what's happened. Oh, that awful Susie! I'll tell Jack exactly what I think of her when he comes!'

But Jack didn't come. Poor Jack! He was just about to start off when Susie and Binkie came rolling with laughter up the drive, the pail clanking between them. When they told him what had happened, he sat down on the front steps and groaned.

'SUSIE! HOW COULD you go to the meeting and pretend to be me? HOW COULD you tell me the wrong time? I can't possibly go to the meeting. I'll have to telephone and apologise for your behaviour – and probably I'll be chucked out of the club!'

'*We* don't mind writing and apologising,' said Susie. 'I don't mind writing a *dozen* apologies – it was *worth* a dozen to crash in on the meeting, and bamboozle everyone – and Binkie was SUCH a good shot with the water!'

'Didn't *anyone* spot that you weren't me?' said Jack in wonder.

'Only Scamper. He growled like anything,' said Susie. 'Oh, I'm going to start laughing again – oh, Binkie, did you think our pail of water would be so *useful*?'

Jack went off in disgust and disappointment. He had been looking forward to the meeting so much. Now he couldn't possibly go. He went to the telephone to apologise for Susie's behaviour – but just as he was about to lift the receiver, the bell rang. It was Janet on the phone.

'Jack? Jack, it really *is* you, not Susie, isn't it?' said Janet's anxious voice. 'This is just to say that the meeting is off for tonight – we're

all rather wet! I expect Susie has told you all about it. No, don't apologise for her, Jack – *you* weren't to blame. But Peter wants me to say the meeting is postponed till tomorrow. Will you come then?'

'Yes. Yes, I'd love to,' said Jack, much relieved. 'Thanks awfully. Actually I was just coming along now, so I'm glad you rang. No – no, of course I won't tell Susie about the next meeting. But why don't you go on with tonight's?'

'We're too wet and cross,' said Janet. 'We'll see you tomorrow, then. Good-bye!'

So, the next night, the Secret Seven met once more, and this time there was no growling from Scamper, for it really was Jack there, not Susie! Everyone made quite a fuss of Jack, for he felt so ashamed and forlorn to think that his sister had spoilt a meeting.

'Cheer up, Jack – it had its funny side,' said Pam, kindly.

'*Had* it? Well, I can't say *I* noticed it,' said Peter. 'However, let's get on with this meeting. Scamper, please keep your ears cocked for any sound outside.'

Scamper at once went to the door, and put his head on one side. Now no one could even *creep* near! Scamper could hear the smallest sound – even the feet of a night-beetle running by on the path outside!

The meeting went quite well. The tin of chocolate biscuits was a great success. There were so many biscuits in it that everyone was able to have at least six – and Scamper had a generous share! He ate his biscuits over by the door, determined not to let anyone come in unless he recognised voice and footsteps!

'Now,' said Peter, when biscuits had been eaten and orangeade and lemonade drunk, 'now – if this club is going to continue properly, we'll have to decide on doing something together.'

'Like helping somebody?' asked Pam. 'Mother says we ought to help some charity if we can't think of anything to do. She says it's silly to have a club that just meets and eats and talks.'

'Well, I like *that*! We've done heaps of things in this club!' said Janet, indignantly. 'Helped people – solved mysteries – and the very last thing we did was to find that dog-stealer. The one who stole the shepherd's sheep-dog, Shadow – and stole Scamper as well, and . . .'

'All right, all right,' said Pam. 'I know all that. I'm only telling you what my mother says.'

'Well, it's fun to have some *aim*, some *interest*,' said Barbara. 'You know – something to think about and puzzle about. Just think of the exciting things that have happened to us – and now here we sit, just eating more and more biscuits, the same as last time. We don't seem to have a brain between us.'

Peter listened, and frowned. 'You know – Barbara's right,' he said. 'We MUST think of something to do. We've plenty of brains between us – we know that. Now – who has any ideas? Speak up, please.'

There was a very long, frowning silence. 'I never *can* think of any good ideas when I'm ordered to,' complained Janet. 'The best ideas aren't ones I think out – they're the ones that come in a flash!'

'Isn't there some mystery we can try to solve?' asked George, 'or someone we can help in some way?'

'Well – there's only *one* mystery I know about – and that's to find out who tied our headmaster's chair halfway up the flag-pole in the school grounds,' said Colin, with a spurt of laughter. 'You can't think how daft it looked there last Wednesday, when we went to school.'

'It would be a waste of time to solve such a silly little mystery,' said Pam. 'In fact, I wouldn't be a bit surprised if it didn't turn out to be that awful Susie who managed to put it there – with her friend Binkie's help!'

That made everyone laugh, even Jack. There was a short silence, and then Colin spoke up.

'Er – I've just thought of an idea – *not* a very good one, I'm afraid. What about trying to get old General Branksome's medals back for him? They've been stolen, you know.'

Everyone stared at Colin in surprise. 'But how on earth could we do that?' asked George. 'Even the police don't know who took them or where they are.'

'The old man lives next door to me,' said Colin. 'And – well – he's very old, you know, and his medals meant a lot to him. And – er – yesterday I saw him telling somebody about them, in his garden – it's next to ours – and it was awful, because tears ran down his cheeks all the time.'

There was a shocked silence. Grown-ups hardly ever cried, and soldiers *never*. And yet the old General had had tears running down his cheeks. How unhappy he must be!

Nobody knew quite what to say. The silence went on, broken by a mournful whine from Scamper, who couldn't imagine why everyone was suddenly so quiet.

'It's all right, Scamper. We're just considering something important,' said Janet, stroking his silky head. 'We're talking about crying, and that's something dogs don't understand. Animals can't cry.'

Scamper whimpered again, as if he quite disagreed with what Janet said. Then George asked a question.

'Can't the General have his medals replaced by the Government?'

'Of course not,' said Colin. 'Anyway, some of them were medals awarded to him by foreign countries. He was a very, very brave man, you know. I simply couldn't *bear* to see him crying

like that. I suppose the thief stole not only the medals, but all his memories – if you know what I mean. Anyway, that's what my father said, and he has one or two medals of his own, so he ought to know what he's talking about. *He* was brave too, in the last war. I *wish* we could get back the General's medals!'

Pam and the other two girls were very much touched by Colin's suggestion. None of them could bear to think of so old and so very brave a man weeping for his lost medals.

'I vote we try to find the medals,' said Pam.

'I don't know how we're going to set about it, but I vote we try.'

'Well – *I* think it's rather an impossible task,' said Peter. 'I do really. *I* vote that we set ourselves some other job as well. Surely the Secret Seven can tackle *two* things!'

'What's the second task to be, then?' asked Jack.

'I vote we keep an eye on nesting birds in Bramley Woods,' said Peter. 'There's apparently a gang going about there, pulling nests to pieces, and killing the young birds – and taking any eggs as well. Well – there are seven of us – what about doing something about it? Scamper would help too!'

'WUFF!' said Scamper, at the top of his voice. So it was settled. The Secret Seven had two tasks – one to look into the matter of the missing medals – and two, to watch for nest-destroyers in Bramley Woods.

'It's a funny mixture, really,' said George, rather doubtfully. 'They don't exactly go together, those two things, do they?'

'Not really,' said Janet. 'But you never know, George, you never know!'

CHAPTER FOUR

Colin does his bit

THERE WAS no time to make any further plans, because there came a sudden clanging of a bell from Peter's house away up the garden.

'Goodness – that's Mother ringing our bell,' said Peter, looking at his watch. 'We must go, Janet. Gosh, I didn't know it was so late. That's the worst of our meetings – the time simply *flies* by!'

'Yes, but wait a minute, Peter,' said George. 'What exactly do we do next? Hadn't someone better go to see the General, and find out a little about the medals – when they were stolen, and how, and all that?'

'Yes. Yes, of course,' said Peter. 'Well, I think Colin should do that as he lives next door to the General, and knows him. Will you, Colin?'

'Er – yes. I suppose it had better be me,' said

Colin, frowning. 'Gosh, I hope he won't mind my asking him questions. He might think me rather inquisitive.'

'Well, after all, he does *know* you,' said Pam. 'You can be very sympathetic, you know – you're good at that – and anyway you *are* very sorry for him. He might not like *strangers* probing into the disappearance of his precious medals, but surely he wouldn't mind *you* being interested.'

'And as for the other thing the Secret Seven mean to do, we'd better arrange with one another to go walking through the woods and look out for anyone disturbing or destroying nests,' said Peter. 'I suggest you all wear your badges when you go – then you can say that you are under orders from your club to protect birds' nests.'

'Do we take people's names, or what?' asked Barbara, looking rather scared.

'Well – you can *ask* for names and addresses,' said Peter. 'You probably won't get them, but it'll upset silly kids if they think people are on the watch for nest-destroyers. After all, there's been a lot about this in the papers, you know, and children *have* been asked to do everything they can to try to stop any cruelty.'

'We'll go about in twos or threes,' said Jack. 'We'll feel braver then!'

'Right,' said Peter. 'Well, make your own plans, please, team up with each other, and do what you can. Report back at the club in four days' time – and if you want to call a meeting before then, for any reason, leave a note down in the shed. Janet or I will see it, for we come down each day.'

'Right,' said Jack. 'Hey, there's your bell ringing again, Peter. You'll get into trouble, you and Janet.'

They all said goodbye. Peter and Janet shut the shed door, and, with Scamper at their heels, raced up to the house.

'*Just* in time!' said Rachel, who was standing with the bell at the kitchen door. 'I've taken in supper, but your father's still washing his hands. Hurry up now, or you'll get into trouble.'

The other members of the club made their ways home. Colin thought deeply as he walked down his road. He dreaded the task of talking to the old General. Suppose the old man thought him inquisitive or impertinent, and shouted at him as Colin had heard him shouting at an impudent tradesman? Suppose he complained to Colin's parents?

'Oh well,' thought Colin, 'I've been given this job to do by the Secret Seven. And after all, *I* put up the idea. But, oh dear – how in the world am I to set about it?'

Colin thought about it in bed that night. He decided that the next morning, when the General took his walk down the garden and back, he would throw his ball over the wall. 'Then I'll sit on the wall, and apologise, and ask if I can slip down into his garden and find my ball,' thought Colin. 'And maybe we'll get into conversation, and I can ask him a few questions. Yes – that's what I'll do.'

So, next morning, Colin took his ball and sat at his bedroom window, watching for the General to take his walk down the garden. Ah – there he was!

Colin ran downstairs and through the kitchen into the garden. He carefully threw his ball over the wall, aiming at some thick bushes well away from the old General. Then he shinned up on to the wall-top, and called cheerfully to the old man.

'Good morning.'

'Oh – good morning, Colin,' said the General, blinking up at him. 'Not at school?'

'No. It's holidays now,' said Colin. 'Look, I'm so sorry, but I'm afraid my ball flew into your garden. May I get it? I promise not to tread on the beds.'

'Yes, yes, of course, my boy,' said General Branksome, leaning on his stick. 'I never mind good-mannered boys coming into my garden. Come along down. And what about a glass of lemonade with me?'

Colin was delighted. That meant a nice little talk! He leapt down, found his ball, and rejoined

the General, who was now walking back to the house. The old man shouted for his cook in a loud voice.

'Emma! EMMA! I have company. Two lemonades, please, and some biscuits. EMMA!'

Emma duly appeared, smiling at Colin, and soon he and the old man were sitting together in the tiny little sitting-room, whose walls were covered with photographs of the General and his soldier friends, and of exciting pictures of old battles. But one space, over the mantelpiece, was bare.

Colin knew why. That was where the General had displayed his medals, glittering there in their velvet-lined case, set with coloured ribbons. The General saw him looking at the bare space, and sighed heavily. The old man began to talk to Colin in his slow voice.

'I expect you heard about someone stealing my medals. To think of a cowardly *thief* owning them! Boy, those medals were won by bravery and daring, by wounds and pain. They were all I had left to show that I was once a fine soldier. I'm an old man now, and nobody thinks much of me – but once people see those medals, ha – they change their minds. They look at me with different eyes. They don't see the poor lame old fellow I am now – they see someone who had DONE things! And now my medals are gone, and I feel old, old, old! I could still feel young when I had them to look at . . .'

To Colin's intense dismay the old man burst into tears, and the boy wished he had never thrown his ball over the wall. He had no right to stir up the old man's grief.

'I'll *find* them for you!' Colin heard himself saying, touching the old man's coat-sleeve. 'I'll find them, I promise you. Don't you fret, you shall have them back. LISTEN TO ME. I'LL FIND THEM!'

The old General was as astonished to hear Colin saying this, as Colin himself was. He shook the boy by the hand with an astonishingly firm grip.

'I believe you, boy! I *believe* you'll find them! Ah, you're a boy after my own heart! You'll be winning medals yourself some day, you will! Ah, here's Emma. Emma, what do you want? Can't you see I've a visitor?'

'Yes. And I can see you've been upsetting yourself about them medals again,' said Emma, patting the old man's back. 'Now, you let the boy go back home, and you have a nice sleep. You didn't have a good night, you know, worrying yourself. You just have a nice lie-down.'

Colin felt in the way. He slid off through the door, and found himself in the kitchen. He stood waiting for Emma to come back. She came in, shaking her head.

'There now – he's having a rest. You shouldn't have talked about the medals. He thinks of them night and day.'

'Do the police know who stole them yet?' asked Colin.

'No. All we know is that somebody got in one night and took the lot – left no finger-prints either. But we do know that he – or she maybe – must have had a mighty small hand, for he had to put his fist carefully through that little hole there – in that broken pane, see – in order to undo the catch and open the window from the inside. I doubt if *you* could put your hand through that broken pane.'

'I'll try,' said Colin. But no, he couldn't wriggle it through the sharp hole without cutting his hand. 'I should have thought that only a small child could get his or her hand through, and reach up to that catch,' he said, puzzled. 'But surely a child wouldn't think of stealing a soldier's *medals*!'

'It's a mystery,' said Emma. 'The poor old gentleman was almost off his head with shock. He's offering a good reward, you know – five hundred pounds! Maybe someone will find the medals hidden away somewhere, and claim the reward.'

'Five hundred pounds!' said Colin, amazed. 'Good gracious – what a lot of money! I wish *I* could find them. But I wouldn't take the reward from the old General.'

'You're a nice boy,' said Emma, approvingly. 'You come and look in my larder and see if there's anything you fancy. I've some fine home-made meringues there!'

'Oh no, thank you very much,' said Colin. But kind old Emma forced two large meringues on him – and they were very, VERY good!

Well – he certainly had something to report at the next meeting. But it didn't really look as if he had any *real* clues to the mystery, except that it was probably someone with a very small hand who had forced that window. And Colin was quite certain that every suspect that came along would have extremely *large* hands! Things always went contrariwise when you were trying to puzzle out something. Colin went red as he remembered how he had promised the General that he would get back his medals for him – whatever had made him say such a thing! He must have been mad! The Secret Seven would be sure to disapprove of such silly talk – and quite right too.

'What's the time?' he thought, and looked at his watch. 'Quite early still. I think I'll hare off to Bramley Woods and join the others there – if only I can find them. I really *must* tell them what's happened. We'll *have* to get back those medals *some*how!'

He ran next door to his own home and popped into the kitchen. His mother was there, very busy.

'Mother – *could* I make myself some sandwiches and go off to Bramley Woods to join Jack and the others?' he begged.

'Well, look – there are some rolls over from breakfast. Butter those, and take some tomatoes,' said his mother. 'Spread the rolls with shrimp paste if you like. And there are plenty of macaroons in the tin, and you can have some biscuits, and . . .'

'Oooh, *thanks*, Mother – wonderful!' said Colin, gratefully. In five minutes he had his lunch in a plastic bag and was off and away. Now to find the others!

CHAPTER FIVE

Bird-nesters – and a rescue

AT THE same time that Colin was talking to the old General, three others of the Secret Seven were on their way to Bramley Woods. They were Jack, Barbara and George. They had decided to picnic there, and, at the same time, keep a watch on would-be-egg-hunters.

'We'll be doing our duty and having fun as well,' said Jack.

'I rather hope we *don't* spot anyone looking for nests,' said Barbara. 'I honestly should be scared to go up and tackle them.'

'We boys will do that,' said George. 'You can just stand by and agree with everything we say. Listen – there's the cuckoo!'

'Perhaps we ought to go and find *him* and tick him off!' said Barbara.

'What on earth for?' asked Jack, astonished.

'Well, you know jolly well that cuckoos go to other birds' nests and throw out their eggs to smash on the ground,' said Barbara. 'Then the hen cuckoo quietly lays her own there instead – and the bird who owns the nest sits on the cuckoo's egg and hatches it out, never thinking that it isn't one of her own.'

'Well – I never knew *that*!' said Jack. 'How in the world did the cuckoo think of such a labour-saving idea?'

'Cuckoo!' called the distant bird. 'Cuckoo! Cuckoo!'

'You can play hide-and-seek by yourself!' shouted Jack. 'And if I find one of your eggs in another bird's nest, I shall take it out!'

'Cuckoo!' shouted the bird, almost as if it were calling Jack names. 'Cuckoo!'

There seemed to be no one about in the woods that morning. Barbara felt rather relieved. It really was too lovely a morning to pick a quarrel with anyone about bird-nesting. They wandered about among the trees, and Barbara picked a great bunch of primroses.

'Well, even if we're not doing a job for the Secret Seven, we're having a nice time,' said Barbara. 'What about sitting down and having an apple each? The birds are singing so madly I'd like to keep quiet and listen to them.'

As they were sitting on the primrosy ground, they heard voices not far off, and soon a little group of three came into sight – all boys about Jack's age. They wandered along, and then Jack and the others saw one boy pointing up into a tree.

'Bother – he's probably found a nest,' said George. Sure enough the boy began to scramble up the tree, and soon he yelled down.

'Blackbird's nest – four lovely eggs in it! Shall I take them all?'

'Take three – one for each of us!' shouted back another boy.

'This is where we butt in,' said Jack, getting to his feet. 'Come on.'

They all went over to the tree, and Jack spoke firmly, but politely.

'I expect you know we've all been asked not to rob birds' nests this spring – there was so much of it last year that the birds have been deserting this neighbourhood and they . . .'

'Listen to him!' said one boy, with a loud laugh. 'Little preacher, isn't he? Give him an egg, Larry!'

The boy up the tree took an egg from the blackbird's nest and threw it straight at poor Jack. It broke and ran down his face.

'I'll pull you down, I'll pull you down!' yelled Jack, in a rage, wiping the yellow yolk off his cheek, and trying to grab the boy's foot at the same time. But that was no good at all. The other boy barged into Jack and down they went, landing in the middle of a thick bush. A bird immediately flew out in fright.

'Ha – there must be a nest there too,' said the third boy. 'Let's look!'

Barbara suddenly felt desperate. She simply could *not* stand by and see a second bird's nest robbed and probably destroyed. She called out in a rather trembly voice:

'We belong to a club that has been given instructions to stop this sort of thing. I shall report you! Look – we're wearing badges. You clear off at once!'

The boy up the tree, and the boys below stared at Barbara in surprise. Then they laughed. 'Look at her silly little badge – it's got S.S. on. I suppose the letters stand for Silly Snoopers! Ha – Silly Snoopers – just about right! Give me your badge – I'll put it into a bird's nest and see what it hatches into!'

He snatched at Barbara's badge, but Jack at once stepped in front. The boy lunged out and Jack suddenly found himself lying on his back in the grass. Barbara gave a scream. The boy up the tree dropped down on top of poor George, and he too found himself on the ground.

'Run, Barbara, run!' yelled Jack, sure that the boys would attack Barbara next. She ran in fright, calling for help, and to her great relief she saw a man lying down reading, under a tree. He leapt to his feet when he saw the running girl.

'What's the matter?' he shouted, and Barbara stopped at once.

'Oh will you come and help? We tried to stop some boys who were taking birds' eggs, and they've got my two friends down and . . .'

'Right,' said the man, and raced off in the direction of loud shouts coming from Jack and George. Both boys were most relieved to see a grown-up suddenly arriving.

The man yelled at the two boys who were now sitting firmly on top of Jack and George. 'Get up! You know bird-nesting is strictly forbidden in this wood. I'll take all your names. Here, you – what's *your* name?'

He caught hold of one of the boys sitting on top of Jack, and yanked him to his feet. But now the three bird-nesters were terrified, and with one accord they ran off at top speed, leaving Jack and George to scramble to their feet.

'Hey – thanks!' said Jack, gratefully. 'Thanks awfully. We were just trying to stop those wretched boys from robbing nests.'

'Are you a club of nature-lovers?' asked the man, seeing the S.S. badges that the three children were wearing.

'Well – we *are* nature-lovers – but our badges mean that we all belong to the Secret Seven Club,' said George. 'And one of the things we've been told to do is to prevent nest-robbing.'

'And a very good thing too,' said the man. 'I'm like you – I love birds and their nests. My word, there are a lot in this wood. I've found about forty already.'

'But you don't take their eggs, do you?' said Barbara.

'Good gracious no!' said the man. 'Actually I mean to write a book about the nests I have found during the last few years.'

'Er – would you care to share a picnic with

us?' asked Jack, thinking that this man might be very interesting. 'We've brought food and drink with us, and we've plenty to spare.'

'Well, that's *very* kind of you,' said the man. He felt in his pocket, and pulled out a large paper packet. 'I've brought sandwiches, too. You have some of mine and I'll have some of yours. Let's sit down over there, on that nice mossy spot – and you can tell me about your club!'

So down they all sat on soft moss, and opened their packages. It wasn't *really* time to have their picnic – but somehow they all felt suddenly hungry.

'This is fun!' said Barbara, and the other three nodded as they munched ham sandwiches, and drank lemonade from small bottles.

'Good thing you were near,' said George, to the man who had come to their help. 'A *very* good thing! Why, those three might have taken our badges away. Would you like to hear about our club? Right – I'll tell you!'

And there goes George, explaining all about the Secret Seven. How proud he is – and how well the stranger listens!

CHAPTER SIX

Tom Smith is rather surprising

'WELL, I must say that I like the sound of your club,' said the man. 'Good badges too – did you make them yourselves?'

'The girls made them,' said George. 'We all meet in a shed with S.S. on the door – and we have great fun.'

'We sometimes help people who are in trouble,' said Barbara, 'and we sometimes solve mysteries, and . . .'

'Good gracious! And what mystery are you solving at the moment?' asked the man. 'By the way, my name is Smith – Tom Smith. Call me Tom, if you like.'

'Well – we'll call you Tom, if you really don't mind,' said Jack.

'Right,' said Tom Smith. 'Now – is the club doing anything besides stopping bird-nesters? Any great mystery being solved, or . . .'

'Well, one of the Secret Seven – Colin – is trying to solve a mystery about a robbery,' said Jack, importantly. 'We gave him that job because he happens to live next door to the man who was robbed.'

'This is all very interesting,' said Tom Smith, taking a currant bun. 'Who's the man who was robbed – and does he know you're helping him?'

'Well – he probably knows by now,' said Jack. 'Colin had to start on the job while we came here to do our bit in preventing bird-nesters taking eggs. I don't suppose you've heard of General Branksome, have you – and his medals?'

Tom Smith looked most astonished. 'You mean the man who had his medals stolen?' he asked. 'You don't mean you're trying to find the *medals*!'

'Well, that's Colin's job – but as soon as he's on to any clue we'll all help, of course,' said George.

'What an extraordinary lot you are,' said Tom Smith. 'Do you honestly think you can find those medals?'

'Well – I hope very much we can, somehow,' said George. 'For one thing, we've heard that there's a reward of five hundred pounds! The postman told us this morning, on our way here.'

'*Is* there?' said Tom, sitting up, looking very surprised. 'What will you do with that enormous sum, if you *do* find the medals?'

'Give it back to the General,' said Barbara at once. 'He's not at all well off, you know. And he's so *terribly* upset at losing his very precious medals.'

At that very moment, a loud yell came to their ears.

'JACK! GEORGE! COOOOOO-EEEEE!'

'Gosh – that sounds like old Colin!' said George, in surprise. 'He must have seen the General, and then raced off to join us. Pity there's not much food left. Hey, COLIN! COOOOO-EEEEEE! WE'RE HERE!'

And in half a minute there was Colin, clutching his bag of food, red in the face, with a huge grin of pleasure at finding his friends. He was surprised to see a stranger with them.

'Hallo!' he said, beaming round. 'So you

haven't finished your picnic. I've brought my own food, but I forgot to bring anything to drink.'

'Plenty of lemonade left,' said George, handing over a bottle. 'What a surprise, Colin! Did you do your Secret Seven job?'

'Yes,' said Colin. He glanced at Tom Smith and then at George. 'Who's your friend?' he asked.

'Tom Smith,' said George. 'He came to our rescue when some bird-nesters turned on us, and we decided to picnic together. So you saw the old General?'

Colin looked at Tom Smith again and hesitated.

'It's all right,' said George. 'We've just been

telling him what the Secret Seven do – and how we hope to help the old General.'

Colin opened his plastic bag and took out a roll and tomato. He began to eat and talk at the same time.

'Yes. I saw General Branksome,' he said. 'It was pretty awful really. You see, he was so *very* upset and miserable. I hated every minute of it. And I said a silly thing – a *mad* thing – to him. I can't think why.'

'What did you say?' asked Jack, curiously.

'Well – I was so awfully sorry for him, that I found myself saying I'd find the medals and give them back to him!' said Colin. 'I mean – actually *gave him a promise*! I can't think why!'

'Well, you *were* an idiot!' said Barbara, shocked. 'Fancy giving a promise you can't POSSIBLY keep! Anyway, I'm sure he didn't believe you.'

'Well, that's the awful part – he *did* believe me,' said Colin. 'He took my hand and shook it very hard, and said "I believe you, boy!" Oh dear – I feel so bad about it now I remember it, that I don't think I can eat anything after all.'

'Don't be an idiot,' said Jack.

'The medals were in a long case, about this size,' said Colin, measuring with his hands. 'I know because I saw the size by the empty space on the wall. Nobody has a *clue* to the thief – except that he must have very small hands, because he had to put a hand through a tiny hole in a window to get at the catch inside.'

'And that is the ONLY clue, you say?' said Tom Smith, suddenly.

'Absolutely the only clue,' said Colin, beginning to eat his roll and tomato at last. 'Gosh, I never felt so unhappy in my life as when the old General was telling me how he loved his medals. He's offered five hundred pounds reward as probably you know – but he's got hardly any money, poor old fellow.'

'I *wish* we knew where those medals were,' said Barbara, looking upset. 'Where can they be hidden? Who took them? If ONLY we knew!'

'Do you know,' said Tom Smith, suddenly, 'do you know – *I* may have a clue to their whereabouts! I'm not sure – but I *may* have!'

The four children stared at him in amazement. Then Colin reached over and pulled at his sleeve.

'Tell us, then,' he said. 'TELL US! Or tell the police. This is very, very important.'

'Well – there may be nothing in my tale,' said Tom Smith, rubbing his chin and frowning. 'Nothing at all. Still, I'll tell you, for what it's worth.'

'Go on!' said Colin, excited.

'Well, as I told your friends here, I love birds and am going to write a book about them,' said Tom Smith. 'And one of my favourite birds is the owl. Now, in Bramley Woods there are many owls – they nest in the old trees here. And the other night I was here, listening to the hoots of this owl and that, lying under a tree, watching the stars shining through the branches – and suddenly . . .'

'Suddenly *what*?' asked Colin, impatiently. 'Don't keep stopping!'

'Suddenly I saw a man creep by me and go to a tree,' said Tom. 'He was carrying something. He didn't see me watching, but I could see what *he* was doing, because he had a torch.'

'And what *did* he do?' asked George, almost holding his breath.

'He lifted up a long slim box – a leather box it

looked like – I saw it by the light of his torch. And he slid it into a hole in the tree-trunk – maybe a woodpecker's hole. Then he made off!'

'What did you do? Didn't you call after him? What was he like? Surely you did *some*thing?' said Colin.

'Was it – was it the box of medals?' asked Barbara.

'I don't know. It was a leather box of some sort, and about the size that holds medals for display,' said Tom.

'Did you go and look in the tree when the man had gone?' asked George. 'What did you find?'

'I went over to the tree and found the hole all right,' said Tom Smith. 'Oh yes, I did that. But my hand was far too big to put down the hole. So I don't *actually* know what the fellow slipped into that tree. Maybe it was those medals – maybe it was something else he had stolen.'

'But if it's the medals they could be taken back straight away to the General!' cried Colin. 'Show us the tree! Barbara here has small hands – she could feel down the hole and see what is there. We know the *thief* had small hands – and how clever of him to slip the stolen goods into a small hole that a large-handed person can't explore. Where *is* this tree?'

'Why should I show you?' demanded Tom Smith in a suddenly rough voice. 'What about the reward?'

'The five hundred pounds! But – surely you wouldn't take that!' said Barbara, horrified. 'You *know* the General is very poor.'

'I'll share the reward with you,' said Tom. 'Four hundred pounds to me – and a hundred pounds to you! Go on – that thief might come back at any time and get the medals he hid – he'd sell them, and they'd be melted down – and that would be the last of them.'

'You'll jolly well show us the tree and let us get the medals!' said Colin, in a fury. 'Where is it?'

'Oh, not far from here!' said Tom Smith, with a grin. 'But that's all I'll tell you! Well, what about sharing the reward?'

'Nothing doing,' said Colin, who seemed to have taken charge of the proceedings. 'Nothing doing at all! For all we know, you may be in league with some thief who hides his goods in holes in trees – some small-handed thief – but *we're* not in league with *you*. We don't intend to ask for any reward – we'll find the medals ourselves. You can't, your hands are too big – and maybe that's why the thief chooses small holes in trees to hide his goods – so that YOU can't rob him of the things he's stolen. What a pair you must be!'

'Now, look here!' shouted Tom Smith, getting up suddenly, and looking very villainous. 'LOOK HERE! I'll show you who's boss! I'll make you see sense!'

And he suddenly caught hold of Colin's coat-sleeve, and pulled him roughly towards him. But the boy slipped free and ran, shouting to the others.

'GET AWAY, all of you! He's dangerous. RUN!'

CHAPTER SEVEN

A very exciting plan

BARBARA WAS very frightened indeed, but the boys were more angry than scared. They all raced off between the trees, and didn't stop until they were out of the woods.

Then they threw themselves down on the grass that bordered the trees, and panted for breath.

'That man – won't – come after – us – will he?' panted Barbara.

'No. Too many passers-by here,' panted Jack. 'My word – who would have thought he'd turn suddenly into such a rogue!'

'Do you suppose he *really* knows where the medals are?' asked George.

'Yes. Yes, I think he does know,' said Jack.

'And I also think he *can't* get the leather case, because of the reason he gave. He really had *enormous* hands – no good for slipping into nesting-holes.'

'I'm sure that he and the thief are in league together,' said Colin. 'Tom Smith, or whoever he is, probably does the planning of robberies or burglaries, and keeps a look-out, and the other man has small hands and finds it easy to do the stealing and the hiding – and is smart enough to hide the stuff in a place that Tom Smith can't get at. Doesn't trust him!'

'What do we do now?' asked Barbara. 'I still feel scared. I want to go home.'

'Well, we simply MUST have a Secret Seven meeting at once about this,' said George. 'The others will have to know everything and we must ALL decide what to do. Let's go to Peter's. Come on.'

So away they trekked, back to the village, and went to Peter's house. They ran down the garden to the meeting shed, and were lucky enough to find Janet there, tidying up.

'Janet! We've got news – big news!' said

Colin. 'We must have a meeting as soon as possible. Where's Peter?'

'Oh dear – he won't be back till three o'clock,' said Janet. 'He's gone out with Daddy somewhere. Is it *really* important? If so, I'll tell him as soon as he gets back, and he'll telephone you.'

'No. Tell him we'll all be here at just after three, unless we hear to the contrary,' said Colin. 'That will save a lot of telephoning. Janet, we've been told where the General's medals are!'

Janet's eyes almost fell out of her head. 'Where are they?' she whispered. But just at that moment her mother appeared, and nobody said a word more about medals or thieves or anything, but just 'Well, see you about three o'clock then!'

They waved good-bye and went up the garden again to the front gate.

'I DO hope Peter will be back by three. This next meeting will be most awfully important,' said Colin. 'Well, see you all later, I hope. Gosh, I feel quite tired after all the morning's excitement!'

'I'll call in and tell Pam on my way back,' said Barbara. 'She'll be excited to know there's a most important meeting on.'

Peter did not telephone, so everyone knew that it was all right to arrive at three o'clock at the shed. Scamper was there to greet them, rushing about outside. He did so love their meetings!

'Hello!' said Peter, welcoming the members. 'I'm longing to know the news. It must be something very important.'

'It is,' said Colin. 'More important than you can possibly imagine. Gosh – I've forgotten my badge!'

'Well – as it's such an important meeting, never mind,' said Peter, generously. Fortunately everyone had remembered the password, so there was no more trouble. Soon they were all solemnly seated on the boxes in the shed, and Peter turned to George.

'Well now – what happened to you and Barbara and Jack and Colin this morning?' he asked. 'You all look so excited. Do you REALLY know where the medals are? Janet said you did.'

'Yes. That's if a man we met in the woods this morning was telling the truth. And I rather think he was,' said George. 'He said that he knew that a man with small hands stole the medals, because he actually watched the man slipping a long, slim leather case into a bird's nesting-hole in a tree – a hole too small for this first man to get his fist into. He said it was probably a woodpecker's hole.'

'So only the small-handed man can get them,' said Peter. 'Well – this *is* news. Did he show you the tree?'

'No – he wouldn't,' said Colin. 'The only clue we got from him was that the tree wasn't very far from where we were picnicking.'

'But as there are DOZENS of trees around that isn't much help,' said Barbara. 'All we know for certain is that in one of the trees nearby, there is a hole made by a bird – or used by a bird for its nest – and into that hole the small-handed thief has slipped the case of medals. It may be halfway down the tree!'

'Looking for it would be like hunting for a needle in a haystack,' said Colin, dolefully. 'We'd NEVER find the hole.'

There was a pause. Everyone looked at everyone else.

'Well,' said Peter, at last, 'has anyone any ideas? Surely the Secret Seven can think of *some*thing between them!'

Janet spoke up, looking rather red. 'Well, *I* didn't hear what this Tom Smith said, of course, but apparently he did say that although he knew the tree, he couldn't get out the medals hidden there because his hands were too big to go into the hole. Well then – what is he going to do? I bet he's going to hide and wait till the other man comes to get them – and then he's going to go for him and snatch the medals! Well – why shouldn't one of *us* go and hide too, and wait to see which tree it is? Scamper could go as well, and . . .'

'And might scare them off, so that we could get at the tree!' cried Peter, in delight. 'Janet, you're too clever for words!'

'Well – I was going to suggest that we should ask the *police* to go and watch as well,' said Janet.

'Oh – I see. No – I think they'd say the reward would have to be paid out,' said Peter. 'And it might go to a police charity or something. Not that I'm against that – but we know the old General is poor, and can't afford to pay out five hundred pounds. If *we* find the medals ourselves, and actually take them out of the tree, the reward is safe. We can say "No thank you, we don't want any reward" – and that's that.'

'Anyway, the police are so BIG,' said Barbara. 'They'd be sure to be seen. We're small.

We could shin up a tree and hide in the leaves like birds!'

'And we'd be *quite* safe with Scamper,' said Pam. 'Wouldn't we, Scamper?'

'WUFF,' said Scamper at once, very loudly. He wagged his tail and looked very proud. So *he* was to be in this adventure too! Ha – what a tale to tell the dog next door!

Everyone suddenly became very excited. '*I* shall go,' said Colin. 'After all, *I* was given the job of solving the medals robbery.'

'And I shall go because I thought of the idea,' said Janet.

'And *I* shall go because I'm head of the Secret Seven,' said Peter.

'Look – don't be silly – we can't *all* go!' said George. 'The thief would spot us – or hear us – as soon as he came near us.'

'How do we know he'd come near us?' asked Janet. 'The tree might be quite far away from anyone.'

'We *know* it's not far from where we picnicked,' said Colin. 'Look – don't let's be silly. We shall mess things up if we *all* go. And I'm not *really* sure about Scamper – he might bark too soon and scare off the thief before he came to the right tree.'

'There's something in that, Colin,' said Peter. 'I think if we take Scamper, he should be some way away, held on the lead by one of us – and not until somebody blew a whistle – me, for instance – would Scamper be allowed to race up and join the fun!'

So they talked – and talked – and planned – and grew more and more excited. At last everything was arranged and settled. Peter repeated their plans for the last time.

'We tell no one at all about this. We meet here when it's dark. Bring warm scarves in case it's cold – and torches – and PLEASE check to see that your battery is good. You don't want to be left suddenly in the dark.'

'It will be moonlight, don't forget,' said Pam.

'I know,' said Peter. 'But clouds may darken the moon – and in any case it will be dark in the wood. Now – when we get to the woods, we keep absolute silence, unless we are able to whisper right into somebody's ear. Understood?'

'Yes,' whispered everyone, imagining themselves to be already in the woods.

'Each of us hides – either up a tree – or in a bush – and keeps watch on all the trees around,' went on Peter. 'Colin will point out where the picnic was held, and then we shall each spread around, and hide in different places, so that if anyone comes that way, one or other of us will see him. There will be no giggling, no noise of any sort that you can help. Understood?'

'Yes,' said everyone again, and the girls felt a little shiver going down their backs. This really was too exciting for words!

'We watch to see what tree the thief goes to, to get the medals from,' went on Peter. 'Then I'll let loose old Scamper, who will go for him and scare him away – and we will examine the tree and remove the medals ourselves!'

'I really do think this is about the most exciting adventure we've ever had,' said Barbara, with a catch in her voice. 'It's quite *dangerous*!'

'Not if you do as you're told,' said Peter. 'And mind – if any one of you begins to feel scared, *keep still in your hiding-place* – don't come out, for goodness' sake – you might spoil everything! Well – that's all. We'll now close this meeting. Remember to be here punctually as soon as it's dark enough. We shan't wait for anyone who is late.'

Everyone at once determined to be on the early side. It would be dreadful to be left out of this most exciting and thrilling adventure!

'If *only* we can find those medals!' said Colin to himself, as he went home. 'And I can take them back to the old General and see his face. I honestly think I want that more than anything in this world!'

Well, keep your fingers crossed, Colin. This isn't an easy adventure – anything may happen, so keep on your guard – and good luck to all the Secret Seven!

CHAPTER EIGHT

Hold your breath, Secret Seven

SUSIE, JACK'S irritating sister, was very curious that night, when she saw Jack fitting a new battery into his torch.

'Are you going out tonight?' she demanded. 'Where are you going?'

'Where I go is nothing to do with *you*,' said Jack crossly. 'Always poking your nose in where you're not wanted.'

'You're going somewhere with the Secret Seven, I know you are,' said Susie. 'Tell me. Go on – you *might* tell me!'

'Certainly NOT!' said Jack, exasperated.

'Oh – then you *are* going somewhere,' said Susie.

'I just *wish* you were a boy,' said Jack. 'I'd

give you such a punch. Stop questioning me.'

'Well – I shall follow you,' said the annoying Susie. 'And I shall get Binkie to come with me.'

'You'll do nothing of the sort!' said Jack, horrified. 'This is a matter for the Secret Seven and no one else. Keep out of it!'

'Well, tell me what it is, then,' said Susie.

Jack stamped away and shut himself into his room. Bother Susie! She had a real nose for anything in the way of a Secret Seven adventure. *Would* she follow him – with that wretched, twitchy-nosed Binkie friend of hers? Well – he'd start pretty early, then he would have time to shake them off.

All the Secret Seven were busy examining their torches that afternoon and going over Peter's instructions in their minds. Scamper couldn't imagine why Peter and Janet were so restless. The time went so slowly for them – it seemed as if the evening would never come!

'Now, Scamper, you'll have to be careful to do EXACTLY what you're told,' said Peter to the eager spaniel. 'You'll probably have to leap at a man and hold him – but don't bite, you understand. And please do be careful not to make *any* noise until I give the word. Understood?'

'Wuff,' said Scamper, happily. Of course he understood!

It seemed a long time to all the Seven before the evening came. Darkness seemed to be later than ever! But then great clouds blew up and the dark night descended quite suddenly. Peter and Janet fidgeted over their supper, and their mother wondered what was the matter.

'Do you feel quite well?' she asked.

'Goodness, yes!' said Peter in alarm. 'Er – the Secret Seven are having a late-ish meeting tonight, Mother, so, as you're going out with Daddy, we'd better say good night to you now. See you in the morning.'

'Well, dear, don't let the meeting go on *too* late,' said his mother. 'Daddy and I will be in just before midnight, I hope – you'll be *fast* asleep hours before that.'

Peter was most relieved to think that his parents were going out. He and Janet were all ready – torches in order, sweets to suck while they were waiting in their hiding-places and warm scarves in case the night proved cold.

The Seven all came together quietly as soon as it was dark. Torches shone out in the garden as the members went down to the shed.

'All here?' asked Peter. 'Yes. Good. All torches alight? Good. Warm scarves? Good!'

They set off together, Scamper at Peter's heels. The moon came out as soon as it grew darker, but they lost its friendly light when they came to the woods, and it seemed very shadowy among the trees.

'Is that footsteps I hear somewhere behind us?' said Peter, suddenly stopping. 'I thought I heard a crack as if someone some way behind had stepped on a twig.'

Jack frowned. Gosh – surely it wasn't Susie and Binkie. No – he really didn't think Susie had seen him slip out of the house. As Peter heard no more suspicious sounds they all went on again, very quietly indeed.

Barbara took Pam's arm. She wasn't scared, but she just thought she'd like to feel someone really close to her. Pam was pleased too! This really was a proper adventure!

Scamper sniffed here and there as he went along. He was delighted to go out for a walk with all the Seven in the dark of night! They came to Bramley Woods, and were soon at the place where they had picnicked.

'Now – we know that the tree where the medals are hidden is somewhere not far off,' whispered Peter. 'We'd all better get into our hiding-places. Anywhere you like, so long as you're hidden. Spread out a bit, so that our eyes can cover a good many trees around here.'

Gradually the Seven disappeared, Scamper too. Peter climbed a tree, and so did Jack. Janet found a fairly comfortable bush, through whose leaves she could easily peep. Pam lay down in some high ferns, hoping nobody would walk over her. Barbara squeezed into the very middle of a bush, where she was so well hidden that not one single S.S. member knew where she was.

'I could almost go to sleep here,' she thought. But, of course, she was much too excited even to shut her eyes!

Colin and George climbed on to a great branch of an old oak-tree, and lay along it, whispering to one another. Scamper lay in some ferns at the foot of Peter's tree, his ears

pricked for the slightest whisper from his master on the branch above.

Nobody could see anybody else. That was good, thought Peter. Very good. It meant that no intruder would see them either.

An owl suddenly hooted from a tree nearby and all the Secret Seven jumped violently. Scamper growled at once, and Peter hissed at him. Scamper stopped growling and lay down again, his ears pricked. What did that bird mean by hooting at him like that?

A rabbit came from a hole and lolloped lazily

across the grass. Everyone watched it in delight. Then it was joined by another, and the two danced around, running here and there, jumping and playing. The moon shone down on them, and Scamper shut his eyes in despair. Rabbits so close – and he dared not run at them! It was too much!

Then a squirrel came bounding along the branch where Colin and George lay, and stopped in alarm to see the boys there. Neither of them moved, and in the end the squirrel decided they were part of the tree, and ran lightly over them, sniffing at their faces inquisitively.

'Oooh – don't tickle!' whispered Colin, and the squirrel leapt away in surprise.

Poor Jack suddenly felt a sneeze coming. His nose tickled and he swallowed violently to keep the sneeze back. It swelled and swelled – and at last exploded into a great big WHOOSHOO!, sending the rabbits down their holes in fright, and making the other Secret Seven members jump almost out of their skins. Peter, not far from Jack, almost fell out of his tree!

'Idiot!' he said, in a loud whisper. 'Don't do

that again, for goodness' sake. I nearly fell to the ground.'

'I couldn't help it,' whispered back Jack, in an aggrieved voice. 'I nearly fell down myself. I say – isn't the moon bright!'

'SHHH!' said Peter, fiercely, afraid that everyone would soon join in the conversation.

There was dead silence once more. Then the wind began to blow a little, and small sh-sh-sh noises were everywhere. The owl descended near Pam's ferns and hooted suddenly again. Pam leapt up with a shriek, making everyone jump in alarm.

'Pam! You'd better go home!' said Peter, in a fierce whisper. 'Go on. Go home!'

Pam subsided into her ferns again, almost in tears. She was NOT going home. Bother that owl! Why did it have to hoot almost in her ear?

Peace descended once again. The owl had gone. The rabbits had shot back into their holes, frightened by the hoot. Nobody sneezed. Nobody coughed. But somebody gave a little yawn!

'SHHH!' hissed Peter. 'I think there's somebody coming.'

That made everyone lie as still as could be. Hearts began to beat fast, and Pam couldn't help hoping that hers wasn't really as loud as it sounded. Bump-bump-bump, it went against her chest.

Yes. Somebody *was* coming! All the Seven – and Scamper too – could hear the sound of soft footsteps padding through the wood. Little twigs cracked now and again, and the newcomer cleared his throat once or twice. Who was it? The thief who had hidden the medals? Tom Smith? Or just a night-walker?

It was *Tom Smith*! There he was, walking in the moonlight, his arms, with their big hands, swinging by his side. Had he come to hunt for the hidden medals – but no, his hands were too big to seek for them in a tree-hole. He would have to wait till the other fellow came, the small-handed man who stole the medals, and hid them in a hole in some tree.

Tom Smith whistled softly as he walked between the trees, passing so near Pam in the ferns that she was half afraid he would tread on her. Then he stopped and looked around carefully. He was not looking for the Secret

Seven, of course, though each of them felt that he was, and cowered more closely in their hiding-places.

'He's come to wait for the thief,' thought Peter, peering down from his tree. 'My guess is that he'll hide somewhere, and watch to see if the man goes to a certain tree. My goodness – this is exciting!'

Yes – it was! Hold your breath a little longer, Seven. Lie quiet, Scamper. Tom Smith is in hiding now – waiting, waiting – waiting – for somebody else to come.

CHAPTER NINE

The Seven are in trouble

Tom Smith went to a broad-trunked oak-tree, and hid himself behind it. He did not know that Colin and George were up in the same tree, just above his head. The boys hardly dared to breathe. Scamper lay still not far off, crouched on the ground, as flat as he could make himself. Everyone was very still – yet inwardly tingling with excitement – waiting to see what was going to happen next.

There came a sudden bark – but not from Scamper! All the Seven pricked up their ears at once. Another dog was coming – maybe the small-handed thief was bringing him – for protection! Perhaps he feared that Tom Smith might be lying in wait for him – as indeed he was.

There came a low, soft whistling, and someone walked into the moonlit patch of grass not far from Pam. Behind him was a large dog.

'Phew – an Alsatian!' thought Peter. 'Let's hope he doesn't sniff out Scamper – he'd eat him up in no time. Gosh – I don't much like this!'

The Alsatian suddenly growled. Had he smelt Scamper – or some of the Seven?

'Shut up, Nabber,' ordered the man with him. 'There's no one about. You can hear rabbits, that's all.'

The man went across the moonlit patch towards a group of big trees, Nabber close behind him, still growling deep down in his throat. Then the watching children saw Tom Smith creep out from his hiding-place. The Alsatian stopped, turned his head, and growled ferociously.

Tom Smith shouted to the other man. 'I'm here, Wily! You get those medals and we'll talk. There's a fine reward out for them now – we'll share!'

'No, we won't,' said Wily, and laughed. 'Ha – I might have thought you'd be on the watch for me. You clear off, else I'll set Nabber on you.'

'Nabber won't touch me,' shouted Tom. 'He knows me. You get those things – go on, now.'

'Come and get them yourself!' shouted back Wily. 'Here they are, see – down in this treehole. Come and stick your big fist in and take them if you want them!'

'You know I can't get my great hand in there,' said Tom, fiercely. 'You were going to double-cross me, weren't you – come here in the dark and take the things out of their hiding-place without me knowing. Oh no, Wily – you just take them out here and now, and hand them over to me. Go on! You don't want to fight a big fellow like me, do you? My fists would make twelve of your dainty little hands.'

Wily began to walk away from the tree he was near. He laughed, and it was such a mocking sound that Tom Smith lost his temper. There came the sound of a loud smack, and lo and behold, little Wily was on the ground! The Alsatian at once flew at Tom Smith, and down *he* went on the ground!

The children watched everything in fear and

astonishment. The only one among them who was enjoying this battle was Scamper. How he longed to rush in and help that big Alsatian.

He couldn't stop himself from barking joyfully. WUFF-WUFF-WUFF!

At once the Alsatian lifted his head and glanced round, amazed. Tom Smith leapt up, and the other man called to Nabber.

'Get that dog!' Nabber rushed at Scamper and bowled him completely over. But Scamper thought it was a game, leapt up, and danced round the big Alsatian, giving happy little whines. He didn't often have the chance of a game with such a big dog!

Peter dropped down from his tree, and so did Jack, both afraid that Scamper might get bitten. 'Scamper! Heel! Come to heel!' ordered Peter. 'SCAMPERRRRRR!'

Nabber the Alsatian was amazed to see two boys suddenly dropping from a tree – and as for Tom Smith and Wily, they stared as if they couldn't believe their eyes. First a spaniel – and now two boys! What on earth was happening in the woods tonight!

Scamper was still darting happily round the surprised Alsatian, who was young enough to enjoy a silly game himself. The two men came over to Peter and Jack, and Tom shook Peter roughly.

'What are you doing here? Snooping? That dog might have bitten you badly – and serve you jolly well right!'

'Take your hand off me!' said Peter, fiercely. 'Yes, we're snooping! *You* told my friends this morning about the medals and how your small-handed friend had hidden them in a hole in a tree somewhere about here. So we came to have a look round, thinking it would be a good thing if *we* got them. They would be handed over to their rightful owner then!'

'And what's more we're going straight back to the police-station,' said Jack. 'I've no doubt that the police will soon catch you both.'

Tom Smith suddenly snatched at Peter's arm, pulled the boy towards him, and looked at his right hand. 'Come on!' he said. '*You're* going to get that case of medals out of the tree for me! Your hand's quite small enough to get right down into that hole. Come on!'

He dragged Peter towards the trees where he and Wily had stood arguing. Scamper flew at him and tried to bite him through his thick trousers. He kicked out and Scamper yelped.

'Don't you dare to kick my dog!' said Peter, furiously. Tom kicked out again, and once more Scamper yelped. That was too much for Janet to bear, and she suddenly leapt out of the nearby bush in which she was hiding, and raced over to the whining spaniel.

'Scamper! DEAR Scamper! Are you hurt?'

Tom Smith and Wily were amazed to see a girl rushing up. 'Look here – how many more are there of you?' said Tom, looking round. 'What *are* you kids doing here so late at night?'

The rest of the Seven couldn't bear to be in hiding any longer, and to the utter astonishment of the two men, Pam jumped up from the ferns she lay in, Barbara pressed out of her bush, and Colin and George dropped down from their oak-tree.

'What *is* all this?' said Wily, taken aback by the sudden appearance of so many children.

'It's the kids belonging to that silly club they told me about this morning,' groaned Tom Smith. 'Look – be sensible, Wily – get that case out of the tree, and we'll both be off.'

'No. I don't trust you,' said Wily, sulkily.

'Right. I'll make this boy get it for me then,'

said Tom Smith, angrily, and pulled Peter to a big, very old tree. There was a hole a good way up the trunk, and he tried to thrust Peter's hand into it, shining a torch so that the boy could see what he was doing.

'Don't!' said Peter, fiercely. 'My hand's too big. Stop it! You're grazing all the skin off. I tell you, it WON'T GO IN!'

'All right!' said Tom, and he grabbed Pam, who was watching in horror. 'Ha – here's a nice small hand. Go on, now – take out the case, girl. Do as you're told.'

'Stand away. You're scaring her,' said Peter, angrily. 'Look, she's trembling. She'll find it much easier if you stand right away. Won't you, Pam?'

He gave Pam a nudge. She pretended to cry, and said, in a shaky voice: 'Stand behind me, Peter. I'm frightened. Keep those men right away. My hand is shaking so much I can't even put it into the hole while they're near me.'

'All right, all right, we'll stand away,' said Tom. 'Now, go on – stick in your hand, feel about for the case, and pull it out very gently.'

Peter whispered in Pam's ear. 'Get the case

out quickly, and give it to me, but *pretend you're still feeling for it.*'

Pam put her hand into the hole, felt the case at once and slid it out easily. Peter took it quietly and opened it. He slid the medals into his pocket, talking loudly to Pam all the time, hoping that the men's attention was elsewhere.

'That's right. Easy now. Got it, Pam? Slide it out carefully, carefully! Those men aren't near you. Don't be afraid! Good girl – here comes the case!'

At these words the men were immediately beside Peter, who handed Tom the empty case, praying that they wouldn't open it. Tom, afraid that Wily would try to snatch it, popped it promptly into his pocket. He turned to go, but Wily caught his arm.

'Wait! What about these kids? They'll race home and tell the police. We need a good start, Tom. And let me tell you this – I'm going to keep you by my side until you hand me half those medals.'

'Oh come now – we can't tie the kids up, Wily,' said Tom. 'No rope, for one thing.'

'Well – we'll leave Nabber on guard,' said

Wily. 'He'll nip any child who tries to run. He'll stay here till morning, if I tell him to.'

'Fine, fine,' said Tom, pleased. 'Tell him, then.'

'Stay, Nabber, stay. All night see, all night. Stay, Nabber!' ordered Wily. 'Round up the kids for me. And STAY!'

'You can't do a thing like that!' cried Peter. But that was exactly what Wily did do! He and Tom Smith set off at a smart walk, and left Nabber behind with the Seven. Nabber whined – but he was absolutely obedient.

He rounded up the seven children, *and* Scamper, and lay down near them, watching warily for any movement.

'This is absolutely the limit!' said Colin, angrily. 'What on earth will all our parents think when they find we're not home? They'll be worried stiff. I'M not going to stay here all night long, anyway.'

And up he jumped and began to walk away down the path. But Nabber was after him in a jiffy. He caught the boy by his coat-sleeve and held on, pulling him backwards to the others.

'It's no good, Colin,' called Peter. 'He's

trained to do this sort of thing. We'll only be dragged back, and maybe nipped if we try to get away.'

'Well, anyway *Peter*'s got the gold medals,' suddenly said Pam, and laughed. 'The men have only got the empty box! Wasn't it clever of Peter to make out I was so frightened, and how lucky they didn't watch what we were doing?'

'Whatever *do* you mean?' said Janet, in wonder.

Peter took out one of the big medals from his

pocket and held it up in the moonlight, laughing. 'Good old Pam! She acted up like anything. She was so quick that I was able to open the box and remove the medals – then shut it, and give it to the men quite empty.'

And then the Seven began to laugh. How they laughed! They had outwitted two thieves and a big Alsatian, and had sent away the men with an empty box – and there was Peter with all the medals safely in his pocket! Well done indeed, Secret Seven! But oh dear, it's NOT very funny to spend a night in the dark woods, with a nasty cold little wind roaming round. And Nabber is *sure* to have you, if you try to escape!

CHAPTER TEN

A long, cold wait

THE SEVEN made themselves as comfortable as they could in the ferns. Scamper lay down beside Peter and Janet, and soon they were quite glad of the warmth of his body, for the night-wind came creeping round, cold and draughty.

'I'm AWFULLY cold!' complained Pam, after a while. 'I really am. Oooh – how I'd love a hot water-bottle.'

'We'd better all get close together,' said Colin. 'Look – you girls get in the middle and we boys will sit round you. That will keep off the wind a little.'

'Thanks, Colin,' said the girls, and were soon squashed closely together, with the boys sitting round them. Peter held Scamper on his lap then, and he really did feel as warm as a hot water-bottle.

'I'll have to lend you round, Scamper,' said Peter. 'You're so nice and warm. You must go and warm up everyone in turn.'

Nabber the Alsatian took very little notice of them. He sat nearby with his back to them, as if watching for Wily his master to return. But at the least sound or movement from the Seven, his ears shot back, and he listened for any sign of escape. Once, when Peter got up to shift his

position a little, and make himself more comfortable, the big dog ran to the group of children, growling and showing his white teeth. It would certainly be no use to try and escape. Nobody would get far with Nabber after him.

'All right, Nabber. We aren't idiotic enough to try and fool you,' said Colin. 'You can go to sleep if you want to!'

But Nabber didn't go to sleep. No – if he had to lie there all night long, he wouldn't close his eyes for a single minute. Scamper closed his, though. He was tired and anxious – something was wrong, and he couldn't do anything about it. He found his eyes closing, gave a little sigh, and went to sleep – but he opened his eyes soon enough when a daring rabbit hopped out of its hole and sniffed at the silent little company.

'Those men will have *plenty* of time to get away,' groaned Peter. 'By the time morning comes, and this Alsatian leaves us, the two men will be miles away.'

'I wonder when they'll discover that the medal case is empty,' said Pam. 'I'd like to be there then. It would be funny to see their faces.'

'I only hope they don't discover too soon that the case is empty, and come racing back to find what we've done with the medals,' said Janet.

'That's not at all a pleasant thought,' said Peter, sitting up straight. 'I hadn't realised they might come back. Gosh – we'll have to look out. Scamper, keep your ears pricked and growl if you hear those fellows returning.'

'Wuff!' said Scamper, at once, and sat up very straight. No more sleep for him!

Half an hour went by, seeming like two hours. The Seven were colder still and Pam shivered so much that the others complained that she made them shiver too.

'Good thing Peter told us to bring warm scarves,' said Barbara. 'At least our necks are warm.'

'I've wrapped *my* scarf round my feet,' said Janet. 'They felt like ice.'

Nabber the Alsatian suddenly rose to his feet, his sharp ears pricked to the utmost. He had been lying some way from the children, nose on paws, eyeing them all in case anyone made a sudden move to escape. Scamper suddenly sat up too.

'Hallo – the dogs have heard something,' said Colin. 'See their ears? Mine feel as if they're pricking up too, but I can't hear anything yet.'

Nabber gave a low growl, but Scamper kept quiet. A sound came in the distance, and Nabber growled again.

'Sounded like a bicycle bell!' said Colin. 'Funny. Who would be cycling to Bramley Woods as late as this?'

Nabber growled again, and looked back at the

Seven as if to say 'Now then – not a sound or a movement, see!' Scamper whined loudly, which astonished the Seven. Why whine instead of growling?

The bell sound came again – yes – it *was* a bicycle bell! The Seven cheered up at once!

'Look – if it's a late-night cyclist, coming this way, we'll all yell our heads off,' said Peter.

'Then maybe he'll stop and we can tell him what's happened.'

'But how can he stop Nabber guarding us?' asked Pam. 'We'll have to warn him about the Alsatian. It would be awful if Nabber went for him.'

'Gosh, yes. I didn't think of that,' said Peter. 'Bother! We can't risk his being bitten.'

Everyone's heart sank. They all listened intently for sounds to come nearer. Ah – there was the ringing of the bell again – *two* bells, surely? So *more* than one person was coming? Perhaps Peter could yell to stop them coming too near – and shout to them to get help of some sort, and explain about the Alsatian. Oh dear – it was all very difficult.

Now *voices* could be heard – children's voices, not grown-ups'! How odd! What children would be cycling at this time of night in lonely roads through the woods?

Jack suddenly gave a shout and leapt to his feet. 'I can hear SUSIE's voice!' he yelled. 'And Binkie's with her! I'm sure it's them!'

'What in the world are they doing cycling

here at this time of night?' said Peter, astounded.

'Susie *knew* we had something exciting on tonight,' said Jack. 'You know how snoopy she is. All right, all right, Nabber, I'm not going to run away, I'm only standing up. Go and lie down, there's a good dog. Oh, Peter, I bet Susie went and looked at my note-book and saw my note there, about meeting in the woods this evening. She threatened to follow me!'

'Well – for *once* in a way I shall be very glad to see that sister of yours, *and* her silly friend, Binkie,' said Peter. 'It DOES sound like their voices. Let's all yell Susie's name.'

And so, echoing through the tall trees overhead and down all the little paths Susie's name went on, on and on in the night. 'Soo-sy, Soooooo-sy, Soo-soo-soo-sy!'

Nabber was amazed at all the sudden shouting. He sat and stared at the yelling children, wondering what to do. Well – they weren't running away – they were only shouting. Nabber lay down again and put his head on his paws. But Scamper went wild with excitement!

He had heard the girls' voices too, and recognised them at once. He raced away from the Seven, down the path, in the direction of the voices. Nabber looked after him, but didn't stop him. Scamper wasn't one of the children. He didn't have to guard *him*!

The voices *were* Susie's and Binkie's! How surprising – and how wonderful! Peter sat and listened to the sound of the voices coming nearer. Never, never had he ever guessed that he would be glad to hear that exasperating Susie's voice!

The two girls had heard Susie's name being called and were now shouting back. 'We're coming! Where are you? Is anything wrong with you? Why are you here so late?'

'We're HERE! HERE!' yelled back the others.

'Come and meet us!' shouted Susie. 'Or flash your torches. It's so dark.'

'Susie, there's an Alsatian dog guarding us. Be careful!' shouted Jack. 'Don't come too near.'

The lights of the two bicycles were now like eyes, coming nearer and nearer. Nabber stood up and began to growl, all his hackles rising on his neck. Jack was afraid for the two girls.

'Don't come any nearer!' he yelled. 'Susie, do you hear me! Get off your bikes and stop. The dog will go for you, if you don't.'

'WHAT DOG?' yelled Susie. But she did as she was told, stopped, jumped off her bicycle, and flashed a torch over towards the Seven. 'Gosh – here you all are, bunched together – you must be frozen!'

Binkie jumped off her bicycle too, and wheeled it towards the Seven. At once Nabber growled and ran out towards her, showing a set of dazzling white teeth. Binkie was terrified.

'STAND STILL!' shouted Peter, and Binkie stood as if she was turned into stone.

'What's up?' called Susie. 'Why is that great dog guarding you? What's happened?'

'Can't tell you now!' yelled back Jack. 'But you can help us a lot. Go and tell the police we're here and can't get away because of this Alsatian. They may know of a dog-handler who can come along and deal with him. Thank goodness you came after us – first time I've ever been glad you're such nuisances!'

'Now, don't you talk like that to *us*!' began Binkie, wheeling her bicycle a little closer.

Nabber gave such a horrible growl that she shrieked in fright and went backwards very quickly indeed. Scamper gave a small piteous whine. He was very, very unhappy to think that he wasn't big enough to fight this determined Alsatian, and send him running.

'Jack!' called Susie. 'We'll do as you say – and we'll be as quick as we can. Goodbye for now!'

'Well – Susie *can* be sensible after all,' said Colin, surprised. 'I always thought she was the world's prize idiot.'

'She's all right really,' said Jack. 'She'll go straight to the police and they'll be here in a jiffy. Susie *can* be really sensible when she wants to.'

The Seven listened to the sound of the girls' shrill voices getting farther and farther away. The bicycle bells rang once or twice, and then no more could be heard. Scamper gave a small whine, and then flopped down on the ground again.

'Cheer up, Scamper. We shan't have to be here all night, after all,' said Peter, stroking the soft silky head. 'I just hope that Nabber has the sense not to fly at a policeman. He's the sort of dog I'd much rather have as a friend than as an enemy.'

Nabber lay down when the two girls had gone and gave a sigh, as if to say 'What a nuisance these children are! Fancy having to guard them for hours!'

'Cheer up, Nabber!' said Colin. 'All nights have to come to an end. This one may end sooner than you think.'

Nabber lay full length and stared at Colin, listening. Then he gave a most enormous yawn, turned round, and sat with his back to them all.

'Doesn't think much of us, that's plain,' said Janet. 'But I like him. Let's sing, to cheer ourselves up.'

So they all sang at the tops of their voices, much to Nabber's amazement. He lifted his head and joined in with the most enormous howls, which made everyone laugh so much that the singing came to an end.

'We'd better listen for the police now,' said Peter. 'They should be here at any moment. Listen – what's that! It's the sound of a car – HURRAY!'

CHAPTER ELEVEN

Nabber meets his match

YES – IT was certainly a car, and it sounded a powerful one. It had extremely good headlights too, which lighted up the woods in rather a weird manner.

It came to a stop just about where the two girls had stood with their bicycles. Then a stentorian voice shouted, 'Are you children there?'

'YES!' yelled back Peter. 'But we daren't move because of the Alsatian dog. He's guarding us. Can't you hear him barking?'

As soon as the police car had switched off its engine, the police heard Nabber barking. What a bark! It echoed all through the wood!

Then suddenly a dark van came up the

woodland road, and drew to a halt just behind the police car.

'That's a *police* van!' said Jack, excited. 'Hey, what a thing to happen to the Secret Seven! Police to the rescue. Gosh – what's that?'

A great clamour had broken out from the van behind the car, and immediately Nabber went quite mad. He galloped round and round the bunch of children, barking and growling in a most unpleasant way. For some reason Scamper joined him, adding his wuffs to the noise.

'This must be a *dream*, I think,' said Barbara, rubbing her eyes. 'It can't be *really* happening!'

But it *was* all real – and so were the policemen that jumped from the first car, and made their way towards the Seven. At once Nabber growled ferociously, and bared his teeth.

'Look out, for goodness' sake – he'll come for you if you walk any nearer!' yelled Colin. 'He's supposed to be guarding us till daylight.'

The two policemen stopped at once, and one called back to the van. 'Big Alsatian loose here, Harris. He'll have to be rounded up before we do anything more. Get your two out.'

'*Two!* Have they brought *two* Alsatians!' said George, in delight. 'Gosh – we're going to see some fun!'

A man stepped from the dark van, holding two enormous, excited, panting Alsatians on a strong lead. They strained at the great leather strap, barking. Then one smelt the scent of the Alsatian near the children, and gave such a blood-curdling growl that everyone's heart began to beat very fast indeed.

'Oh please – they won't *fight* Nabber, will they?' shouted Janet. 'He's not a bad dog, really he isn't. Don't let him get hurt, will you?'

'He won't get hurt, missie, if he behaves sensibly,' called the man holding back the two dogs. 'And keep that spaniel close to you, will you? Don't let him move if you can help it. And all of you keep absolutely silent, and absolutely still while my dogs get to work.'

Janet promptly took Scamper, who was quivering with excitement, on to her knee and held him as tightly as she could. She needn't have worried – Scamper had no intention of getting mixed up with dogs so much bigger than he was!

The seven children never forgot what happened in the next few minutes. Not one of them had seen a trained dog-handler at work – dogs and man understood one another so well that it seemed as if the two police dogs knew what was in their master's mind almost before he had given a command.

'I'm going to let my dogs go now,' shouted the dog-handler. 'Don't scream or shout, you children. They won't harm you at all – they won't even notice you. They'll just round up that other dog, and bring him to me.'

In dead silence, the children watched everything in the light given by the car-lamps. Janet held Scamper so tightly that he whined. The two police-dogs pattered slowly up to where they were all sitting, and fixed their eyes on Nabber, who now crouched behind a big tree, his tongue hanging out, his eyes gleaming in the car-lights. As he watched the two dogs, he began to growl.

'Round him up!' shouted the dog-handler. 'Get to work, Sasha! Now!'

And at the word 'NOW!' Sasha gave a great leap forward, then sideways, and was suddenly right behind the surprised Nabber.

'Now you, Vanya!' yelled the man. And there was the second dog, facing Nabber, ready to fly at him, whichever way he turned. Nabber tried to dodge this way and that, showing his teeth all the time – and then suddenly he leapt right over the dog facing him, and disappeared into the woods.

'FETCH HIM!' yelled the handler. There was the noise of a scrimmage in the ferns some way away, and then Nabber came flying back to the children. He leapt right over the whole bunch of them as they sat there, alarmed – and then up raced Sasha and Vanya, leaping over them too. The girls were scared, but the boys enjoyed it.

'Quite a circus!' whispered Peter to Jack, as they watched the three dogs tearing round, leaping, dodging, Sasha and Vanya snapping at Nabber, sometimes disappearing through the trees for a few seconds, but always coming back to the handler, who still shouted instructions to them from time to time.

Quite suddenly Sasha leapt on Nabber from behind, and got him by the scruff of his neck. Nabber howled and tried to get free.

Then he began to whine piteously.

'Right. Drop him, Sasha!' said the handler. 'Bring him to me. DROP HIM! He won't run away any more. Nabber – that's your name, isn't it? Come here, then. Good dog, then, come here.'

And to the children's intense surprise, the fierce Nabber, head hanging down, limping a little on one leg, went obediently to the dog-handler. On each side of him, came Sasha and Vanya, their tails wagging victoriously. The man patted Nabber on the head, fondled his

ears, and then, as Nabber rolled over in delight, tickled his tummy. Sasha and Vanya watched solemnly, and waited for their own reward of pats and praise.

'WELL!' said George, watching in amazement. 'Wouldn't I love to be able to handle dogs like that? I'll jolly well train to be a dog-handler as soon as I'm old enough.'

A police officer came up to the children. 'Well, now the fun's over, you'd better see if you can all squash into our car and we'll run you home,' he said. 'Those two girls who came to tell us about the trouble you were in, will be glad to know you're safe – and so will your parents, I should think. But now – how was it you were here at night, with that dog on guard so that you were his prisoners? And whose dog is he?'

And then, in the car, the whole tale came out, of course – about the stolen medals – the man called Tom Smith who had told them they were hidden in a tree-hole too small for his big hand to slip into – and how they, the Seven, had had the idea of coming to find the medals themselves – and had run into trouble.

By this time they were almost out of the

woods, and in the lane that led to the main road. The police officer had listened carefully to the story, without interrupting. 'Do you know the names of these men – and can you give us a description?' he asked. 'I think they're the two that we are after for a series of burglaries – and other things!'

'Well – one said his name was Tom Smith – and he called the other man Wily,' began Peter – and then stopped suddenly as they passed by a little inn called the Hare and Hounds. He caught at the policeman's arm.

'Could you stop the car? I rather think that was Tom Smith rushing out of the front door of that inn, with Wily after him. I'm pretty sure Wily was shouting, too. I expect they've quarrelled – about the medals!'

And then, to the policeman's surprise, Peter began to laugh and laugh. No wonder – for he had had the medals *safely in his own pocket*! But the police didn't know that – yet! Peter was determined that the old General should have the medals delivered to him personally by *Colin* – for that was what Colin had promised the old man.

The car slowed and stopped just by the two men. Tom was fending off Wily, and both men were shouting angrily.

The police van in front noticed that the second car had stopped, and it stopped too, and reversed. The police officer in the second car jumped out and ran to the driver of the first one.

'We'll pick up these two fellows for questioning,' he said. 'Hurry up. I rather think we've got the men we've been looking for. That Alsatian in your car – Nabber – belongs to one of them.'

And then, to Tom Smith's surprise, and to Wily's horror, the two policemen bore down on them and took them firmly to the van, where they were put in with the three Alsatians. Nabber was too thrilled for words to see his master, and covered him with licks. Wily was amazed to see his dog. 'I'm dreaming!' he said, stroking Nabber. 'Yes, I'm dreaming! Nabber, I left you with those kids – and here you are with the police. Yes, I'm dreaming. Good thing you're in my dream, too, Nabber – you'll look after me, won't you?'

'I'm beginning to feel *I'm* dreaming too,' said

Janet, as the two cars went on their way again, with seven children, four dogs, two policemen, a dog-handler and two prisoners. 'Let's hope we don't have to pick up anyone or anything else!'

The two cars swept into the village and stopped at a corner. 'Now you kids tumble out,' said the police-officer. 'Time you were all in bed! We'll be round tomorrow to see you. Tell your parents there's nothing to worry about – we're very pleased with our night's work. I only hope we'll find the old General's medals in Tom Smith's pocket.'

You won't! They're still in *Peter*'s pocket! Only ONE person is going to give back the medals to General Branksome – and that's Colin, of course!

CHAPTER TWELVE

Well done, Secret Seven

ALL THE children's parents were extremely relieved to see them safely home. They each said the same thing.

'WHERE have you been at this time of night? And WHAT have you been doing? You are NOT to do this kind of thing – we were TERRIBLY worried!'

Susie had also been very worried. She was very glad indeed to see her brother Jack coming in at the front gate. She had been watching anxiously for him. Binkie was with her, also watching.

'There he is!' shouted Susie, rushing to the front door. 'In a police car, too. The police must have been quick off the mark, Binkie.'

'Yes. But I was pretty scared when we went to the police-station, and told them about the Seven and that horried Alsatian dog guarding them,' said Binkie. 'I'm sure that first policeman we saw didn't believe us.'

'Jack! Did the police rescue you?' shouted Susie, and to Jack's great surprise, she rushed to him and gave him a bear-hug. 'I *was* so worried!' she said. 'What happened?'

Jack told her how the police cars had come, and how the wonderful dog-handler and his charges had tamed the ferocious Nabber. 'I *wish* I'd seen him!' said Binkie. 'You Secret Seven do have marvellous times together.'

'Well – this adventure was pretty scary sometimes,' said Jack. 'Honestly I don't know what we'd have done if you and Binkie hadn't come along – snoopers though you are! By the way, Susie, how *did* you know where we'd gone? *Did* you look in my note-book? I expect I made a note there about where we were going. You *shouldn't* read people's private writing.'

'I know,' said Susie. 'But I get so curious when I'm sure that you and the others have something exciting on hand – and when I found your notebook on the floor, well – I just couldn't help myself. I picked it up and read it and then I telephoned Binkie, and we took out our bikes to follow you. Just as well we did!'

'Well – it was, as it happened,' said Jack. 'But it was a *snoopy* thing to do, Susie. Only girls do that sort of thing.'

'Aha! Does Janet snoop then? And Barbara and Pam?' cried Binkie.

'No. Of course not,' said Jack, and hurriedly changed the subject. 'Anyway, it was jolly good of you and Susie to help us when we were in such a fix. I was scared stiff of that Alsatian. I think his name's a very good one, don't you – Nabber! I'm glad he didn't nab *me*!'

The next morning was rather exciting. The police saw all the Secret Seven, and listened to their story of the finding of the hidden medals in the tree. 'But what we'd *really* like to know,' said one of the police officers, 'is where on earth the *medals* are! They weren't in the pockets of either of the thieves, and they seemed as puzzled as we were to know where they had disappeared to. Tom Smith produced the medal case out of his pocket – but when he

opened it, no medals were there! It was empty! We searched both men, but found nothing.'

'Strange,' said Peter, solemnly, and Janet nodded.

'Very curious,' said Barbara and Pam, trying not to giggle.

'*Most* extraordinary!' said George and Jack.

'It would be interesting to know where the medals *are*,' said Colin, frowning.

The others grinned behind his back, marvelling that Colin could keep such a straight face. They all knew that he had the glittering medals in his pocket, carefully wrapped in tissue paper that he had taken from his mother's cupboard. Peter had handed them to him just an hour ago, and had told him that he, and he alone, must give them to the old General, as soon as he had a chance.

Colin had been a little uneasy when Peter handed him the medals. 'You're SURE that it doesn't matter *me* handing them back to the General, instead of the police taking them to him?' he said, anxiously. 'They won't be angry with me, will they? It's only because we don't want him to have to hand out a large reward that he can't possibly afford.'

'Look – you go and give them to him as soon as you get a chance,' Peter said. 'I know we *all* had a share in discovering them, Colin – but it was *you* who promised to bring them back.'

And now the time had come to take the medals to the old General. Colin felt decidedly nervous. 'How shall I explain it all?' he thought. 'How can I tell him all about Tom Smith and Wily and Nabber? I shall get into a terrible muddle, and so will he. I think I'll just push them into his hand.'

He didn't go over the garden wall this time, but knocked politely at the front door. Emma opened it. 'Why, it's you, Colin,' she said.

'Come away in. The police are here, but they'll be gone in a minute.'

'The police? Oh, then I'll come another time,' began Colin, in fright, but Emma hustled him along the passage and into the sitting-room.

The old General was there, and so were the police officers who had driven the police cars the night before.

'The boy from next door to see you,' said Emma, pushing Colin before her. General Branksome beamed at Colin.

'Good morning, Colin. I've something to tell you! The police have brought me back the case my medals were in, and they are rather hopeful of getting back the medals too. What do you think of that?'

'We have NO idea at present where the medals are,' said one police officer, hurriedly. He turned to Colin. 'Perhaps you can make the gentleman understand that we really haven't much hope,' he said. 'We just thought he'd like the case back, medals or no medals.'

'Colin here said *he'd* bring me back my medals,' said the General, beaming round.

'And I believe him. He's that sort of boy – does what he says he will do. Fine type of lad. Lives next door to me.'

'May I have the medal case, please?' asked Colin, solemnly, and the General picked up the empty box and gave it to him. Colin opened it. Then he put his hand in his pocket, and took out the little bundle of medals wrapped carefully in soft tissue paper. He unwrapped them one by one and put them gently back into their places in the leather case.

The two policemen couldn't believe their eyes! They watched Colin, too amazed to speak. The medals! Shining gold medals! Perhaps they were dreaming?

The General watched too, a beaming smile on his wrinkled old face. 'Ha, what did I tell you?' he said to the two surprised men. 'I told you this boy said he'd get them back – I knew he'd keep his word. He's that kind of boy. HE shall have the reward! FIVE HUNDRED POUNDS!'

'No, thank you,' said Colin, hurriedly. 'No, THANK YOU VERY MUCH. We don't want the reward. That's why I was told to bring them back to you myself – so that you wouldn't have to pay out such a large sum of money. We – er – we enjoyed getting them back very much indeed.'

The two police officers stared at Colin in silence. They had been pleased at least to bring back the empty medal case – but this boy had brought back the medals themselves!

'Er – we'll have to ask you a few questions, boy,' said one of the officers. 'The first thing is – where did you and your friends get these? We've hunted all over the place for them.'

'They were in a hole in a tree,' said Colin, beginning to enjoy himself.

'Indeed – and did *you* put them there by any chance?' asked the officer.

'Oh! no. Wily put them there,' said Colin, solemnly. 'He has such small hands, sir.'

The General had now put all his medals back into the case, and had hung it up in its usual place over the mantelpiece. He went to the door and shouted, looking ten years younger.

'EMMA! I have company! Bring something to eat and drink. EMMA, MY MEDALS ARE BACK!'

The two police officers couldn't stay to chat and eat and drink with the old man, so they said goodbye, patted Colin on the back, and went, looking rather puzzled.

'Pity that boy didn't come and tell *us*,' said the first officer.

'No. No, I think it was right that *he* should take them back to the General,' said the second officer. 'It does seem that *he* promised to find them for him.'

'Odd, that,' said the first officer. 'He can't possibly have known where they were.'

'Well – if people very, very much want to do something for somebody else, somehow they find a way,' said the second officer. 'Haven't you ever noticed that?'

The old General was as happy as a boy all that day, and how he enjoyed hearing the whole story from Colin! He told Emma about 'that boy, Colin' a score of times. 'If only I could think of something to give him – and something for his friends too!' he said. 'You see, Emma, they won't take the reward. There are seven of them – and two girls helped besides, called Binkie and Susie – and I believe there's a dog called Run-Along, or something like that.'

'Oh, you mean Scamper!' said Emma. 'Now look, General, what do you yourself feel most proud of, what do you most love looking at and wearing?'

'Well, my medals, of course,' said the General.

'Right. Then why don't you give those children medals too – just little ones – with their names on one side – and with "FOR BRAVERY" the other side. Because, from all I've heard, they *were* brave!'

'Emma, you *do* think of fine ideas,' said the

General, pleased. 'Of course – just the thing! Medals! And I'll ask if I can go to their next meeting and pin them all on. Ha – what a fine time we shall have!'

So next week there is to be an extra-special meeting down in the shed, with the General presiding, and pinning on ten medals – yes, Binkie and Susie are to have one each too. Peter says that is only fair.

Ten, did I say? Let me see – seven for the Secret Seven, one each for Binkie and Susie. That's nine.

'Wuff-wuff-wuff!' Oh, of *course*, Scamper, the tenth one is for *you*. You were in the adventure, too. How proud you will be when you race about with a medal swinging from the front of your collar! Congratulations to you and all the Secret Seven – and may you have many more adventures!

Fun for the Secret Seven

Contents

CHAPTER ONE

A meeting, please!

'PETER! PETER, where are you?' shouted Janet, racing up the stairs.

'Here – in my room,' called Peter, appearing at his door and looking very cross. 'I'm tidying it up. Dad looked in this morning, and wanted to know if I *liked* living in a pigsty! He said the pigs were tidier than I am!'

'Well – he was about right,' said Janet, looking round the room. 'Do you *ever* pick anything up when you drop it? Goodness, what's this mess on the carpet – something stuck to it?'

'Oh – so *that's* where my nougat went!' said Peter, scraping a sticky mess off the carpet. 'Good thing Dad didn't tread on that – it would have stuck to his shoe for ages!'

Janet gave a delighted chuckle. 'You really are dreadfully untidy, Peter,' she said. 'I suppose I'd better tidy up your room for you before Daddy comes back again.'

'What did you want me for?' asked Peter, still scraping. 'Ooh – it's horrid, this. What a waste of a nice bar of nougat.'

'Listen, Peter – a note came through the letterbox just now. It's addressed to "Peter, Head of the Secret Seven". So it's for you. Who is it from, do you suppose?'

'Oh, one of the others wants something, I expect. Maybe a meeting of the Seven for some reason,' said Peter, tearing open the envelope. 'Yes – it's from Jack. Listen. He says:

'"*Dear Peter,*

Will you call a meeting? I have had a strange request for help from Bob Smith. He's in our class at school, you know. He didn't say much except that he needs our help badly. He's pretty upset. Perhaps the Secret Seven can help him – he's a good friend. Anyway – isn't it about time we met again, before we all forget we're the Secret Seven?

"Jack."'

'Oh dear!' said Janet. 'He sounds rather high and mighty, doesn't he? I suppose you ought to call the meetings more often, Peter. They're great fun.'

'Well, after all, so many of us go away during the summer holidays, it's hardly *worth* holding meetings then,' said Peter, rather red in the face. 'I wonder what's up with Bob Smith – and why he wants *our* help.'

'We've only got a week or so before the autumn term begins,' said Janet. 'You'll have to be quick about the meeting if we want to get all the members there.'

'Right,' said Peter. 'I'll scribble three notices

of our next meeting, and you scribble two, Janet.'

So up they went to the playroom, and when Mother looked in to see why in the world they were both so quiet, she found them busily writing out the notes. She looked over Peter's shoulder, and read what he had written.

Please come to a meeting in the shed at half past two this afternoon. No one admitted without the password. We have to discuss something important. Bob Smith will be at the meeting. I shall ask him five minutes later than anyone else, in case he overhears the password. Wear your badge else you won't be allowed in.

Peter

'Well!' said Mother, in surprise. 'Whatever does Bob Smith want help for? I think . . .'

'Oh, Mother – you shouldn't have read that bit,' said Janet. 'It might be something secret. It *will* be fun to have another meeting! Peter – do you remember the password?'

'Of course!' said Peter. 'But I bet *you* don't.'

'No – I don't,' said Janet. She grinned at Peter's solemn face. 'It's all right. I've written it down in my diary, so all I have to do is to look it up. Ha! Ha! You were sure I'd forgotten it. *You* tell me what it is – I bet you don't remember, either!'

'Yes, I do,' said Peter, crossly. 'As if the head of the Secret Seven could forget his own password! It's Scamper's name – just "Scamper". Easy!'

'Thanks!' said Janet, with a grin. 'Now I shan't have to look it up. Lovely password – Scamper!'

'Wuff!' said a surprised voice, and Scamper raised his head from the floor, where he had been lying waiting for the others to take him for a walk. He leapt up and ran to Peter, putting his lovely golden head on the boy's knee. Peter patted the soft, silky head. 'You coming to the meeting too, Scamper? All right. Half past two sharp. So don't go rabbiting after dinner, because you won't be let into the meeting-shed if you're late!'

Scamper gave a small whine, and licked

Peter's hand. How *could* he be late when he was going with the two children?

'Did you remember to tell Jack in your note that he could bring Bob Smith to the meeting?' asked Janet.

'Yes. But he's to tell Bob to come five minutes *after* us, so that he doesn't hear the password, and so that we can ask Jack what's up with Bob, before we see him,' said Peter, folding up the last of his notes. 'Come on now – we must deliver these at once, so that the others have plenty of notice about the meeting.'

They were soon on their way and went the round of Peterswood, popping the notes into various letterboxes. 'I do hope everyone will be

able to come!' said Janet. 'Shall we take something to eat and drink? It's much more fun then.'

'Yes. Mother will help with that,' said Peter. 'I'll buy some sweets too. Luckily I've got some pocket-money left.'

'Well, NOT nougat, then,' said Janet, firmly. 'Even Scamper is tired of licking up dropped pieces. Buy some boiled sweets. They take ages to suck, and everyone likes them. Oh, I *am* glad we're to be the Secret Seven again! Come on, Scamper! We haven't finished yet!'

It wasn't long before all the notes had been delivered. They caused quite a bit of excitement. As soon as one had been dropped into Jack's letterbox and he had run to pick it up, he read it and raced after the two children going out of his front gate.

'Hey! Are we *really* going to have a Secret Seven meeting this afternoon? Three cheers! I thought the Secret Seven had gone west!'

'Then you were a fool,' said Peter. 'As soon as I had your note I arranged a meeting at once. We're all back from holiday now, and it will be fun. Bring Bob Smith with you, as I said in my letter. We'll try to help him if we can.'

'I don't really know what's up,' said Jack. 'He didn't tell me. But I do know he's been going around looking pretty miserable. I bet we *can* help him!'

'See you at the meeting, then,' said Peter. 'I suppose you've lost your badge as usual?'

'I have *not*!' said Jack, indignantly. 'Just because I lost it once, you think I'm going to lose it always! And *I* didn't lose it then; my sister Susie took it, as you very well know.'

'Well, don't shout at me,' said Peter, grinning, 'else that awful sister of yours will hear you and try to come to the meeting with Binkie, that silly, giggly, twitchy-nosed friend of hers.'

'They're both going to a party,' said Jack, thankfully. 'So they'll be well out of the way. I do wonder what old Bob wants to tell us, don't you?'

'Well, we'll soon find out,' said Peter. 'By the way, Bob is to wait outside till we're ready to have him in. I put that in the note. Leave him some way off so that he can't hear what our password is.'

'Right,' said Jack. 'I've got the password

written on the back of the calendar in my room. It's . . .'

'Well, don't shout it out, or Scamper will come rushing to you!' said Peter, with a chuckle. 'So long, Jack!'

When Peter and Janet had delivered all the notes, and had a little talk with each delighted member, they went home, *just* in time for dinner! Their mother called them as they went in at the garden door.

'Wash your hands, quick!' said Janet. 'I'll wash mine with you to save time. Put the bottle of boiled sweets where we can see them in case we forget them. All right, Mother – we're coming! JUST coming!'

Scamper raced into the dining-room with them, hungry as a hunter. Where was his bowl of meat? Ah, there it was. Good old Rachel, she had got him JUST the kind of meat he liked best. Soon he and the two children were all eating hungrily. Mother laughed.

'Anyone would think that you two and Scamper hadn't had a meal for weeks!' she said. 'Scamper – don't gobble so. You'll choke! There – I knew you would!'

However, Scamper went on gobbling and had finished his dinner almost before the children had eaten three mouthfuls. He went to his rug and lay down, yawning. Ah – that was good! He wouldn't mind eating another whole plateful! He thought it was a pity that nobody ever offered him a second helping. He shut his eyes sleepily.

'Hey – don't you fall asleep, Scamper! You have to come to a Secret Seven meeting after we've finished dinner,' called Peter.

'Woof!' said Scamper, sleepily. He shut one eye and kept the other open.

'Funny to be half asleep and half awake like that,' said Janet. 'What's in that package over there, Mother?'

'Just a few new-made buns for the hungry Secret Seven!' said Mother, smiling. 'I made them this morning.'

'Mother, you're great,' said Janet, and gave her a hug. 'I don't know why food tastes so nice when we all sit in the shed and talk. But it does.'

'I've some boiled sweets too,' Peter told his mother. 'And I dare say one or two of the others will bring something. Gosh – it *will* be fun to have a meeting again.'

At a quarter past two Peter and Janet left the house with Scamper, and went down to the meeting-shed. They carried the buns, the sweets and four bottles of ginger beer.

'Let's hope one of the others brings something to drink too,' said Peter. 'Four bottles of fizz won't go far between seven of us on this hot afternoon.'

'Eight, you mean. Bob will be there,' said Janet. 'Nine, with Scamper!'

'Woof!' said Scamper, agreeing, his tail wagging hard.

Nobody had yet arrived at the shed. There it stood, the letters S.S. on the door. Janet pushed it open and looked inside. The shed was quite tidy, but it needed a dusting. She took the duster from a shelf and flicked it round the seats and little table. She put the bottle of sweets and the ginger beer on the table, and looked to see if the plastic mugs on the shelf were clean. What fun it was to be welcoming the Secret Seven members once more!

A knock came on the door and Peter spoke at once. 'Password, please.'

'Scamper,' said the voice, in a low tone. And then other footsteps came and low voices spoke the password, 'Scamper! Scamper! Scamper! Scamper!'

Scamper the spaniel was delighted to hear his name so often. He began to bark loudly, and leapt excitedly up at everyone as they came in.

'Sit, Scamper! I shan't use your name for a password again if you get so excited,' said Peter. 'Anyone would think *you* were the head of this meeting, not me! SIT!'

Scamper sat, his tail wagging beneath him. Oh, how good to see all the Seven again – Colin

– Pam – Barbara – George – and Jack – and Peter and Janet, of course.

Jack had come in alone, leaving his friend Bob outside as he had been told. They all sat down, and Peter sat on the stool at the head of the little table.

'Welcome!' he said. 'I'm glad you all remembered the password, and said it quietly. Now, Jack – will you please tell us exactly why you have called this meeting? But first call in Bob – he'll have plenty to tell us!'

CHAPTER TWO

Bob Smith's story

THE SECRET Seven meeting was soon under way. Jack stood up to tell everyone why he had wanted it called that afternoon. He looked worried, and spoke earnestly.

'Thanks, Peter, for calling a meeting so quickly. You see, it's on account of something Bob told me. I saw him looking pretty worried yesterday and I asked him what was the matter and he told me about Old Man Tolly.'

'Old Man Tolly? The old man who lives in that tumbledown house on the top of the hill?' asked Peter, in surprise. 'What's the matter with him? *You* tell us all about it, Bob!'

'Well – he lives all alone except for an old horse and his dog,' said Bob. 'You've often seen that nice old horse – brown and white, with a lovely mane. Tolly's cottage has two rooms, and he lives in one, and Brownie the horse lives in the other.'

'Goodness – how odd!' said Pam.

'Not really,' said Bob. 'He loves that old horse. When old Tolly worked for the farmer on the hill beyond, he and the horse were together all the time. The horse was strong then, and could pull carts and wagons and goodness knows what. Then one day it pulled a heavy cart-load of stones down that big hill – and the weight made the cart run too quickly for the old horse, and it ran into his back legs and lamed them. So he wasn't any use for heavy work any more.'

'What happened then?' asked Peter.

'Well – the farmer blamed Tolly for the accident,' said Bob, 'and he said the horse was only fit to be shot, *he* wasn't going to buy fodder for him, if he couldn't work for his keep.'

'Oh! How DREADFUL!' said Pam and Janet together, tears coming suddenly into their eyes. 'Poor old horse!'

'Well, Tolly was heart-broken,' said Bob. 'He was sure that the horse-doctor – that vet man called Whistler – could make the horse's legs right again, and he called him in.'

'Good for him!' said Peter, and the others nodded.

'Well, it might have been good for the vet, but it wasn't very good for old Tolly,' said Bob. 'The farmer wouldn't pay the vet's fees, though the horse was his, and told him to send the bills to *Tolly* – and they came to over a hundred pounds!'

'Goodness!' said Peter, startled. 'What a lot of money! Surely Tolly couldn't pay all that?'

'Of course he couldn't,' said Bob. 'Apart from his pension, his wages are so low – he's old, you see, and can only potter about, and now he's really ill with worry. I was up there yesterday – my mother sent me up with some eggs – he used to work for us once, and we're fond of him . . . And he told me all about it then. He showed me the vet's bills too. Whew! I do think the vet might have kept his fees low.'

'My father won't use that new vet,' said Peter. 'He says he's too young and too hard.

He hasn't learnt to love animals properly yet. He wouldn't even come to one of our cows one night when it got caught in a fallen tree. Poor thing, the tree had fallen on top of it in a high wind, and it was scared stiff, and one of its horns was broken.'

'Will he have old Tolly sent to prison if he can't pay?' asked Pam, in a frightened voice.

There was a shocked silence as the children thought of poor old Tolly all alone in prison, without the dog he loved, and without the horse whose friend he was.

'Have you come to us for advice?' asked Peter, at last. 'Is there something you want us to do?'

'Well – I simply don't know what *I* can do to help, and I thought you Secret Seven might have some ideas,' said Bob, looking round at them all, his face very worried indeed. 'How can old Tolly pay that bill? Where can he put the old horse now, so that the farmer won't take him away? I'm no good at solving puzzles like these – but I thought you Secret Seven could help somehow.'

There was a little silence, and then Janet

spoke up, her eyes bright. 'Well, to begin with, I'm willing to empty my money-box to help to pay the vet's fees. Then that farmer won't have to worry about those, the mean old thing!'

Everyone began to talk at once.

'Yes, that's the first thing to do – pay the bill!'

'No! *I* think the first thing to do is to find somewhere to keep the old horse safely. Don't let's have him left anywhere near that horrid farmer!' That was Pam speaking, very, very fiercely!

'Yes – Pam's right,' said Peter, knocking on the little table for silence. 'Pam's absolutely right. We *must* get the old horse out of that farmer's reach if possible.'

'Well, that would be easy – if we knew anywhere he could live,' said George. 'He's a big horse – I know him. He would need a decent stable, not a tiny shed.'

'Peter – wouldn't Dad let us have a place in one of our stables?' said Janet. 'Just for the time being, anyway. Dad wouldn't charge a penny, I know!'

'That's a good idea of yours, Janet,' said

Peter. 'But remember, if we take that old horse away and stable him somewhere here, that horrid farmer may come after us, and charge us with stealing the horse!'

'Oh my goodness!' said Pam, scared. 'What can we do then? We've simply *got* to do something!'

'Well – we could find out how much the farmer wants for the old horse, and see if we can possibly earn enough money ourselves to pay for him,' said George. 'We've all got money-boxes. And if we hadn't enough, we could jolly well earn some more. What's the use of the Secret Seven if they can't tackle a thing like this?'

Bob flushed red with excitement. He stood up and spoke earnestly to the meeting. 'I KNEW the Secret Seven would do something. I KNEW they would. I think you're great. Well – I really can't TELL you what I think!'

'That's all right, Bob,' said Peter, kindly. 'We are all glad you came to us about this. We'll do SOMETHING, you may be sure – with your help too, of course. You can't be a member of the Secret Seven, but you can certainly be a helper with us, in whatever we do about this problem.'

Peter then addressed the meeting. 'I shall ask my father to let us have a stall in one of the old stables. Bob, will you please find out from Mr Tolly exactly how much the vet's bills are – there may be more than one – and if possible *get* the bills – and we could ask the vet if he would be generous enough to take some of the fees off, so that there won't be so much to pay.'

'Well – whatever the bills come to, even if the vet reduces them, old *Tolly* can't pay,' said

Bob. 'He's only got his pension – his work is just a few jobs here and there for the odd pound.'

'We want someone to clear up our orchard,' said George. 'I'll ask Dad to get old Tolly, and pay him.'

Ideas came thick and fast, and everyone was sorry when a knock came at the door, and Peter's mother put in her head. 'I'm afraid the meeting must soon stop. It's getting quite late!'

'Right, Mother,' said Peter, and waited till his mother had gone. 'Now listen, everyone. This needs a lot of thinking about – a lot of considering. I am now going to close the meeting, and everyone is to go home, and think HARD this evening to get some kind of good idea about this problem. Come back here tomorrow morning at ten – you too, Bob – and we will sort out all our ideas and decide exactly what the Secret Seven can do to help – decide the BEST way to help. Tonight I shall ask my father about a shed or a place in our stable. That's the most important thing at present.'

'Oh, thank you, Peter,' said Bob, his face red with delight. 'I shan't worry tonight. I know you'll all think of something super by tomorrow. I wish I had your brains.'

'You've got something better, Bob,' said Pam, unexpectedly. 'You've got a VERY kind heart!'

And then out came the new buns and the fizzy ginger beer. Out came the boiled sweets and some chocolate and biscuits brought by Jack and Pam. What a feast!

When the little feast was over, the meeting broke up, and everyone went their way. They certainly had something to think about that night – something very difficult – something that had to be dealt with at once.

Good old Secret Seven! Think hard, and see what *you* can do!

CHAPTER THREE

Plenty of ideas

AT EXACTLY ten o'clock the next morning there came a number of raps on the Secret Seven shed door. The password, which was still 'Scamper', was whispered through the door and Scamper, who was inside with Peter and Janet, cocked his ears with pleasure every time he heard his name. He gave little whimpers of delight as the Seven filed in and took their places.

Last of all came Bob, out of breath with running. 'Had to do a job for my father,' he panted. 'Hope I'm not late.'

'We wouldn't have started without you,' said Peter. 'It's important that everyone should be here. Now, the meeting will begin. Stop chattering, please, Pam and Barbara.'

The two girls stopped at once, and faced Peter. This would be a worthwhile and exciting meeting, and they didn't want to miss a word!

'The meeting has now begun,' said Peter. 'Please address any remarks to me, because if we all start chattering to one another, we won't get anywhere. First of all, I must tell you that Janet and I have asked our father about a place in one of our stables for Mr Tolly's horse.'

'He said yes,' began Janet, eagerly, and stopped as Peter spoke to her sternly.

'Janet! *I* was speaking!' said Peter. 'Please let me finish.'

'Sorry,' said Janet, going red.

'I'm very pleased to say that my father was sorry for Mr Tolly, and said that the farmer who owns the land on the hill was very hard-hearted,' said Peter, and everyone nodded in agreement.

'He said he would willingly give us a place in our biggest stable for Mr Tolly's horse – and he wouldn't charge him anything. BUT – he said he thought that Janet and I might like to keep the stable clean ourselves, so that the stable man wouldn't have to do any more work than usual.'

'I'll take my turn at that!' said George. 'No reason why you and Janet should have to muck it out all the time. I'd be pleased to come every Saturday.'

'Look – we'll *all* take turns,' said Colin. 'All of us. Why not? We've taken this thing on together, and we'll jolly well all share in everything. I'll come each Monday after tea.'

'And I'll come whenever I can,' said Bob. 'I must take my share. I'd like to – if the Secret Seven don't mind me butting in.'

'I think we'd better make you a temporary member,' said Peter, and the others nodded at once in agreement. Peter solemnly knocked on the table.

'I propose that we make Bob Smith a temporary member, until the matter he has brought to us is well and truly settled,' he said, in a very grown-up voice. 'Does the meeting agree to this proposal?'

Everyone agreed very loudly indeed. 'And now,' said Peter, 'I'd like to hear whether Bob has found out exactly what amount the vet's bill is.'

Everyone looked so solemnly at Bob that he felt he must stand up. He looked round at the others, feeling just a little wobbly on his legs. 'Er – thank you very much for saying that I can be a temper – tempory – well, whatever it is – member. It's really kind of you. Yes, I did go and find out about the vet's bill. I went to Mr Whistler and I just asked him straight out how much old Mr Tolly owed him.'

'What did he say?' asked Peter.

'Well – he looked a bit startled, and asked me

why I wanted to know,' said Bob. 'And I told him we were sorry for Mr Tolly, because he was afraid the horse would be shot if the bills weren't paid – and that we would do our best to get at least *some* of the money pretty soon, if he would wait.'

Bob paused for breath and everyone looked anxiously at him. What had the vet said?

'Well, the vet was very decent. He said that he hadn't understood that Mr Tolly would have to pay – and he said he would reduce the bill by half – and that I was to tell Mr Tolly he wasn't to worry, and that he'd still go on coming to see the horse and how it was getting on – and not charge him a penny more!'

'That was marvellous of him!' said Janet, her face one big smile. 'Did you tell him *we* would pay the bill ourselves, if he'd let us have time to earn the money?'

'Yes, I did, and he looked so astonished that I was sure he didn't believe me. He asked me what on earth we thought we could do to earn so much money. Even if he halved his bill, there would still be nearly eighty pounds to pay. He said that Brownie's legs had needed daily attention for some time, and that was why his fees had mounted up. Actually they came to one hundred and fifty pounds – and half that would be seventy-five pounds!'

'What did you say?' asked Peter.

'I just said that we'd talk it all over at our next Secret Seven meeting, and I'd let him know. I didn't like to make big promises on my own,' said Bob. 'But I did ask him if there was anything *he* wanted done, which one of *us* might be able to do.'

'*Was* there anything?' asked Colin, eagerly.

'Yes. He said his delivery boy – you know, Fred, who delivers any medicines for animals that the vet has seen during the day – well, he said Fred wanted two weeks' holiday to go and stay with his grandfather, and if any of us would like to do his rounds each evening, he'd pay him the same as he pays Fred.'

'How much is that?' demanded three or four voices at once.

'He pays him one pound fifty a night,' said Bob. 'So I said *I'd* take Fred's place while he was away. You see, if I earn one fifty a night for a whole fortnight – let's see, that's fourteen evenings at one fifty a time – er – er – that would be . . .'

'You're no good at figures, Bob!' said Jack. 'You would earn exactly twenty-one pounds – and let me tell you, that's a lot of money! It would probably pay over a quarter of the vet's bill – gosh, this *is* a bit of luck, your getting the errand boy's job for a fortnight. If you get tired of it, one or other of us will take over for you.'

'I shan't get tired of it,' said Bob. 'The only thing is, I have to have one evening off a week to go to choir practice, so one of you can take over then.'

'Right. I'll do that evening for you this week,' said Peter. 'Gosh – fancy being able to knock off over a quarter of the vet's bill like this! Good for you, Bob. You did well.'

Bob sat down, his face flushed with pride. He decided to be the best errand boy that the vet had ever had. He decided to ask him if he could clean out the kennels in which the vet kept dogs when they were boarded out with him. That would be more money earned, perhaps. And would the vet like him to feed the cats each morning – or . . . Bob's mind ran on and on, and when he finally came to the end of his thoughts about the vet's jobs, he felt almost like a vet himself!

Yes – it WAS fun to be one of the Secret Seven – or was it the Secret Eight now? Bob made up his mind to be the best member they had ever had. His heart swelled with pride. A member of the Secret Seven – and the vet's errand-boy too – he really was getting on in the world!

CHAPTER FOUR

Mr Tolly – Brownie – and Codger

IN BED that night Peter thought about the successful meeting the Secret Seven had had that day. He and Janet were to clean out the stables in return for shelter for Mr Tolly's horse. The others would do their share of stable-cleaning too. Bob was to be an errand-boy – and they could take turns with him, if he wished. There must also be quite a bit of money in the money-boxes belonging to the Secret Seven. That would help to pay for fodder for Mr Tolly's horse. He would need something more than grass to eat . . .

Peter's thoughts grew muddled, and he found himself drifting off to sleep. He was happy. His worries about Mr Tolly and his horse began to fade, and his eyes closed in sleep. His last thoughts were of money-boxes – he must tell the members to open – their – to open their – money-boxes. Yes, their money-boxes! And then, with his thoughts getting all twisted up, he slid into dreams – strange dreams in which Mr Tolly, dressed as a little horse, ran about delivering medicine bottles to all the cows in his father's field!

Next morning Peter and Janet set off with Scamper to find Mr Tolly in his little tumble-down cottage on the side of the hill. He must be told the good news – that the Secret Seven were going to earn money to pay Mr Whistler's bills. Then he wouldn't worry any more about having to sell his brown and white horse.

There was the little cottage, whitewashed, leaning against the hill. Down in the valley below were flocks of sheep, every nose touching the grass in the meadow as they fed. Playing round them was Codger, a nice but ugly little mongrel dog, who thought his master was the finest man he had ever seen!

'Mr Tolly isn't with the sheep,' said Janet,

looking down the hill. 'He must still be in his cottage. Let's go and see.'

As soon as the little mongrel dog saw the children going towards his master's cottage, he came tearing up the hill at top speed, barking fiercely. Who was this, DARING to go to his master's house? He barked round their ankles, and Janet was a little scared.

'Don't take any notice of his barking,' said Peter. 'He's only behaving like a good little watchdog. Come on, little dog – take us to your master!'

Tolly wasn't in his cottage. The children knocked and knocked, and finally tried the door. It opened. They peeped inside. The cottage was trim and neat and clean. Old Tolly couldn't keep it like that himself, surely! They went round to the back, where there was a small garden with a vegetable plot, and a washing-line. Taking down a sheet was a thin little woman.

'Hello!' said Peter, surprised to see a woman there. 'Is Mr Tolly in?'

'No, he's gone to do his shopping,' said the little woman. 'Look, isn't that him coming up the hill? Run and take that heavy bag from him. I've just finished his washing.'

The two children went to meet Tolly, and he was very glad to give them his bag of shopping. His dog raced to meet him in delight, barking loudly. His beloved master was back again! Scamper, who was with the children, jumped up eagerly at the old man, too, for he knew him well. Tolly laughed and sat down on an old wooden seat he had made years ago.

'That hill!' he said. 'It gets steeper and steeper, I do declare! I'll get my breath in a minute. So you've made friends with Codger, have you? Fourteen years old, he is, and as good as any five-year-old. Down, Codger, you'll be tearing the young lady's jumper!'

'Oh, I don't mind him jumping at me,' said Janet. 'I think he's a fine little dog. He's got such a nice face too. I like dogs with nice faces. Some have rather fierce ones.'

'Aye, he's a good, kind little dog,' said Tolly. 'When I broke my leg two years ago, and lay out there in the rain, at the bottom of the hill, Codger stayed with me all night long. Wet and cold he was, and miserable, but he warmed me all he could, and when morning came, he left me and went to the farmer's place, and pulled at his coat to make him come to me. Aye, he's a good little fellow. My old horse is a good one too. I'm a lucky man I am – I've got the two best friends a man can have – a horse and a dog. Come and see the old horse.'

They went to the old, draughy, tumbledown cottage. A brown and white horse put his great head out over a half-door, and nuzzled Tolly and the children. He tried to nuzzle Codger too, but he couldn't reach far enough down over the door. Codger leapt up and licked him on the nose. Tolly undid the door catch and the great horse lumbered out at once, keeping close to Tolly.

The old man fondled both the dog and the horse, talking to them gently. He looked tired and ill. The little woman in the house came out with a cup of tea for him.

'Here, old man, you come and sit down after that long walk up the hill,' she said. 'You leave your horse be, he's all right. You're forever a-mothering of him, and bless me if he doesn't mother you too – or try to. Look at him nuzzling about you! Or maybe you've biscuits in your pockets?'

'Yes, yes, I have – and old Brownie knows it,' said old Tolly.

'You'll have to look after him well!' said the little woman, jokingly. 'There's horse-thieves about this district, so I've heard. One of these nights they'll come and steal your old horse away!'

The old man sat down suddenly on a near-by seat. He looked upset. 'HORSE-thieves!' he said. 'They'd like my Brownie, they would. He's got good blood in him, Brownie has. The prizes he won when he was younger! I've got them all in the cottage. You must see them, youngsters, you must see them. Horse-thieves you say,

Ma'am, horse-thieves! Where can I put my Brownie?'

'If you think there *is* any danger of Brownie being stolen, bring him down to our stable,' said Peter. 'We had already decided it would be a good place for him to live, if you'd like him to. He can't go back to that horrid farmer. And you could bring your little dog Codger too – see how he has made friends with Scamper! Goodness, he can run as fast as our spaniel – faster! Do come down to stay at the farm, and bring the horse and dog. You can have the shepherd's old hut. He's not using it now the lambing season's over.'

'Yes now, Mr Tolly, you do that,' said the little woman, who had been listening all the time. 'You take your horse down to Peter's stables, and Codger as well. If you can have the shepherd's hut, you'll be right grand in it! Go on now – I'll get my sister Agnes to keep an eye on you and the cottage – she'll do your shopping for you too. You go this very minute, with the children. I know their mother, I've worked for her at spring cleaning time. She'll maybe give you an easy job or two to do. And while you're gone I'll give your old cottage a really good turn-out!'

The old man didn't quite know what to say. Peter took his arm. 'You come with us. You *couldn't* let Brownie be stolen. He'll be safe in our stable. Come along, come along!'

Before old Tolly quite knew what was happening he found himself being led down the hill to the valley below, where the farm lay, peaceful and lovely. Brownie and Codger followed behind. Tolly was quite bemused and certainly more than a little scared by the mention

of horse-stealing. His long memory stretched through the years, bringing back vivid pictures of his sorrow when horse-stealers had taken six of his most-prized shire-horses.

'Aye,' he suddenly said, out loud. 'Aye! I reckon old Brownie would be safe down in your father's stables, youngster – and I'll be sleeping alongside him. Maybe your dad has got a few jobs I can still do. I don't like working for Mr Dinneford now – he's hard, he is, and he doesn't understand that animals have got to be loved as well as fed. He doesn't love even a lamb – no, nor even his dog. And he was going to shoot old Brownie who has worked for him for years – just because he hurt his back legs working for him.'

'Don't worry any more,' said Peter and Janet together. But the old fellow went on worrying. 'You see – old Brownie's really Mr Dinneford's, not mine – but I've cared for him all the years, and he's like a brother to me now. It nigh broke my heart when that heavy-loaded cart ran on to his poor old back legs!'

Janet was upset to see a large tear run slowly

down old Tolly's rough cheek. She slipped her arm through his. 'Don't you worry any more,' she said. 'You shall come and live in our shepherd's old hut, and when Brownie is in our stable, quite safe, you'll feel happy.'

'The vet can come and see his legs and make sure that they get quite better,' said Peter, saying everything that he could possibly think of, to comfort the old fellow. But this didn't bring any comfort at all! Tolly stopped as if he had been shot, and pulled his arm away from Peter. He faced him, looking very scared.

'The vet – Mr Whistler?' he said. 'I'll have to go to prison if his bill isn't paid. That's what Farmer Dinneford told me! Go to prison, and leave my dog and Brownie behind! Mr Dinneford wouldn't bother to feed them – they'd be dead when I came out. No, no, young man, you are very kind, I know, but I can't have that Mr Whistler any more. Mr Dinneford, he says I'm to pay those bills, because he reckons it was my fault that old Brownie got so badly hurt. He knows I think of Brownie as my own – I've looked after him so many years now, and we've worked together for the master, and . . .'

He broke off and bent down to pat Codger, who was very worried because his master sounded so angry and so sad. He licked old Tolly's hand gently.

'How much money would Farmer Dinneford ask for Brownie?' said Peter.

'Old Brownie wouldn't fetch much now,' said Tolly. 'He's old, and now that his back legs are weak, because of that heavy cart running into them, he's not all that good for farm-work. But he still costs as much in fodder, and those vet-bills are a real worry. I'm so afraid that Mr Dinneford will think he's not worth his keep any more, and – and will have him shot.'

'Don't you worry,' said Peter, feeling quite desperate. 'We'll see that he's not shot. Er – Janet and I are thinking of buying him ourselves – and then he'd be quite safe, wouldn't he?'

Janet stared at Peter in the greatest surprise. *Buy old Brownie?* Where would they get the money from? What would their father say?

Would Farmer Dinneford sell him? Yes, probably – but he would put a good price on the old horse if he thought that somebody else wanted him! She tugged at Peter's arm.

But he shook off her hand impatiently. 'Well, Tolly, what price do you think Farmer Dinneford would want?'

Tolly had been so surprised when he heard Peter say that he and Janet were thinking of buying Brownie that he just couldn't say a word. He gaped at Peter, opening and shutting his mouth like a fish.

'Well – what price *would* Brownie be?' asked Peter again. 'One hundred pounds, do you think?'

'Oh more than that, youngster, more than that,' said Tolly, finding his voice. 'Why, you and your sister couldn't possibly buy a horse. What pocket-money do you get – two pounds a week?'

'We've saved up quite a bit,' said Peter. 'But we couldn't pay more than one hundred pounds between us.'

Tolly shook his head. 'Mr Dinneford would say two hundred pounds, maybe more,' he said. 'Though I'd say myself that's too high a price for an old horse with poor hind legs. The legs might go weak any day, and then Brownie would be no good at anything except cropping the grass.'

Peter gave a heavy sigh. What a pity he wasn't grown up. He could then do as his father did – go to the bank and take out quite large sums of money. He could buy Brownie easily then!

'Er – my friends and I are going to help to pay the vet's bill – Mr Whistler's account,' said Peter. 'I thought I'd tell you now, to save you worrying. We haven't got the money yet, but we're earning some. One of my friends is working for the vet at night – taking round medicines. He reckons he'll earn twenty-one pounds in two weeks.'

'And Dad says that if we muck out the stable and keep it decent when Brownie comes, he'll provide the old horse with free fodder,' said Janet. 'And I bet the others are thinking of some more ideas too. So don't you worry, Mr Tolly. We'll be sure to get enough money for the vet – and Brownie will be safe from harm down in our stable – he'll be happy with the other horses. They're nice ones – they don't kick or anything like that. I'm sure they'd love Brownie.'

'Oh, what's all this you're saying?' said old Tolly, staring at the two children in surprise. 'I've heard your dad is a good kind man, and it's certain that he's got children like himself! All right, Brownie and me, we'll leave Mr Dinneford. I'll leave Brownie with you, and come to sleep in the stables at night – and work out a week's notice with Mr Dinneford. He'd be after me if I left at a moment's notice. And don't you say a word to anyone about my Brownie being with you – in case the farmer hears of it and comes after him. Not a word!'

'We certainly won't!' said Janet. 'Look, here we are. Let's go into the stable. We've already chosen a stall for Brownie, next to a nice kind horse – and there's plenty of good fresh hay for him!'

They all went into the stables, Codger wagging his tail fast. This was quite an adventure! Brownie gave a little whinny, as he smelt the horsey-smell, and tapped on the floor with his foot as if to say, 'Very nice. Very nice indeed!'

There were no other horses in the stables. They were all out working, or feeding in the fields. Brownie began to nibble at the fodder in his stall.

'Look at that now. He's at home already,' said Peter. 'Good old horse. You're safe here, Brownie. Come down tonight and sleep in the stables with him, Mr Tolly. You'll *both* be safe – and happy – and warm.'

CHAPTER FIVE

The police vet calls

AFTER TEA time that same day Tolly arrived at the farm to sleep in the stables with Brownie. He found the children's father waiting to see him.

'Ah, Tolly – I see you've put your horse – or it is Mr Dinneford's horse? – safely in our stable,' he said. 'Well, I'm glad to see it there, as, according to the children, there's a chance of it being shot because of the accident it had. But – er – what does Mr Dinneford say about this arrangement? I hope you told him. I've examined the horse's hind legs myself, and they're not right yet, by any means. I doubt if he'll be any good for farm-work now. Nice horse too – good strong animal.'

'Yes,' said Tolly, anxiously. 'The vet said his legs *would* get better, he thought – but slowly. And I expect you know that Mr Dinneford, he's impatient, and he won't keep any animal that can't do much, but eats its head off all the time, and costs money in fodder, and . . .'

'Yes, yes. I know his reputation,' said Peter's father. 'Well, I'm willing to let you and the horse sleep in my stable at night, in order that Brownie shan't be shot. If you've given notice to Mr Dinneford, I'll take you on myself, as I'm short of a man. You'd do general work – horses – sheep – field-work, and so on. What about it?'

'Well, I'm very, very grateful indeed. I've given in my notice, and Mr Dinneford, he was so angry with me, and said I must go at once. And he said he was going to shoot Brownie tonight, as I wouldn't be there to see to him and his bad legs. They have to be rubbed at night with this liniment stuff that the vet gave me. The master, he said the vet was making a fuss, but this stuff is good. It's helping Brownie's legs, I know it is.'

'Right. Keep it then, because you'll be in

charge of Brownie, with the two children as your helpers,' said Peter's father. 'And don't worry about the horse – he'll be safe here. In any case I shall get in touch with the police in case of any trouble.'

'Right,' said Tolly and touched his cap. Well! he thought, this is the kind of man I want to work for. Knows his own mind – kind – sensible – forthright. And I've got old Brownie too. What'll happen if Mr Dinneford comes after him, though?

But Peter's father had thought about that. He had telephoned the police and had told them about his engagement of Tolly, and the fact that the man had brought the horse to him.

'Dinneford was going to shoot it – or so he says,' said Peter's father to the police sergeant who answered the telephone. 'I'm willing to buy it off him at a reasonable price to save its being shot. The horse's hind legs are no good at the moment, so he's a bit of an old crock – but they may mend. Shall I get the vet in to say what he's worth at the moment – in case Dinneford makes a fuss, and puts an enormous price on the horse?'

'No, sir – don't get Mr Whistler,' said the police sergeant. 'Better get our own police vet – he'll be here soon to look over the police horses we have for our two mounted police – the ones that go round the markets when there are great crowds about. Wonderful what a horse can do, when crowds gather, and won't clear away. People scatter like sheep when the police horses gallop up! I'll ask our vet to go down to your place tonight, sir. Thank you. Good evening, sir!'

So that night the police vet came along,

smart and spruce, and very quick. He examined old Brownie from head to tail, from shoulders to hooves, looked into his mouth and even inside his ears! Tolly stood near by, looking very anxious. He didn't know *what* to think!

If he says the horse is fine, strong as can be, healthy and able to work hard, it'll mean he's worth a lot of money, and I shan't be able to pay the price for him, he thought. And if they think he's a poor old horse, because of his accident, I'll not dare to work him, in case of harming him. I don't know WHAT to wish for!

The police vet went to talk to Peter's father when he had finished.

'Well, sir,' he said, 'he's a good horse, as good as ever he was. But he does need gentle handling, sir. He's a bit nervy. That may be because of the accident he had, of course. If he could be handled now by someone he knows and trusts, he'll soon be all right – but don't let any stranger handle him, sir – he'll get more nervy, and not be a bit of use to anyone in a few months' time. Gently does it, sir, with that horse. I'd take him off your hands myself, if I could. He's a beauty!'

'Thanks very much indeed, Sergeant,' said Peter's father, pleased. 'You've said more or less what I myself thought. What would he be worth now, if anyone bought him?'

'Well, sir, not much if you sell him to a stranger, or to a bad handler,' said the vet. 'He seems happy enough here. Why don't you keep him? You wouldn't get more than one hundred and fifty pounds for him now, with those damaged back legs. But a patient owner, who wouldn't work the horse at all for say, six months, would find he had a first-class horse at the end of that time, strong, willing and as good as ever!'

'Fine, fine!' said Peter's father, and the two children, who were listening, squeezed each other's arms in delight. Now Brownie would be bought – and kept. And Tolly would come to them, and have a good job, and be with the horse he loved!

How they hoped that Mr Dinneford wouldn't want Brownie any more! Anyway, he'd be safe with them for some time, recovering slowly in their stables!

CHAPTER SIX

Brownie gets a new home

WHEN THE police vet had gone, Peter's father and mother, Mr Tolly and the two children and Scamper went into the summer-house for a good long talk.

'We have to decide straight away what we can do about Brownie,' said Mr Tolly, anxiously. 'He can't go back to Mr Dinneford, to the farm. He'd be worked and worked there, or shot, maybe, and he's not as strong as he was. Have you examined his hind legs? What did *you* think of them?'

'Well, it's a toss-up, Tolly,' said Peter's father. 'With careful, friendly handling Brownie might be as good as ever in six months' time – but his hind legs are definitely not strong enough for hard work yet. But who's going to keep a horse for six months or maybe longer and not work him – and possibly find at the end of that time he's no good at all? It would be money down the drain for anyone who bought him then.'

'Would you tell Mr Dinneford that?' asked Tolly, anxiously. 'If he'd sell Brownie now, while he would go cheap, I'd buy him. I wouldn't work him at all for six months, and I'd be glad to buy his fodder and see to him. I shall soon be leaving the farm up on the hill there – I can't work for Mr Dinneford any longer, and anyway, I've given in my notice. I could go somewhere with Brownie, and get a job for myself, and see that the old horse was quiet and happy till his legs were quite mended.'

'You know you can stay here, Tolly,' said Peter's father. 'You're an old man now, you want a quiet job, with not too much heavy work. If you like to come to me and see to my horses for me, as I said, you'd be welcome. Sleep in the stables, or in the shepherd's old hut, or out on the hills, wherever you please.'

'Thank you kindly, you're a real gentleman,' said Tolly, warmly. He turned to Peter. 'Yes – you're lucky, you are – that's a *real* gentleman your father is, and just see that you grow up like him, young man. You won't go far wrong, then!'

Peter grinned, delighted at this praise of his father. 'Are you going to buy Brownie from my father?' he said. 'That's if Mr Dinneford will sell him, of course – and I bet he will if he thinks he can't work Brownie for ages.'

'Young man, I haven't even fifty pounds to my name!' said Tolly. 'Else I'd buy him this very minute. What with having to pay out for my rent and fire and light and clothes and food, and with having to help an old invalid sister of mine, I don't have as much money to spare as you have! But I'm going to ask your dad if he'll keep back so much of my wages each week, so that when I've about one hundred pounds saved, I can buy Brownie for my very own. That's if Mr Dinneford will sell the horse to your father, of course!'

'Mr Tolly, would you let us share Brownie with you, if we pay *half* the one hundred pounds for him?' asked Janet. 'If he's coming to live here with us, I'd so like to think we could share him.'

'You can share him all you like, when he's mine,' said Tolly. 'You can consider him half yours and half mine. He'd like that. He likes children. You don't need to pay me.'

'Oh but we must,' said Peter. 'We shouldn't feel as if he really *was* half ours, if we hadn't paid something for him. We'll buy the half with the bad legs, if you like, so that you can have the best half.'

'Well, whatever will you say next?' said Tolly, astonished. 'Now look – you save up and buy half of him if you badly want to. I know how you feel. I feel like that myself. I shan't be happy till I've paid over that hundred pounds to your father and then can look at old Brownie and say to myself, "You beauty, you're mine. I've worked for you, and cared for you, and paid for you – and now you're mine to look after for the rest of *your* life!" There's something about horses that just *gets* me. And old Brownie – well, he's – he's . . .'

'The best horse in the world!' finished Peter,

with a laugh. 'I feel rather like that about Scamper, our dog. You know – best dog in all the world! Are you, Scamper? Rachel says you're just a scrounger with muddy feet and an inquisitive nose. But *I* think you're the Best Dog in the World!'

'Woof!' said Scamper, wagging his tail very fast indeed. 'WOOF!' He ran to Peter and licked first one of his hands and then the other. Peter patted him lovingly. 'Old fuss-pot! You do love a bit of petting, don't you? Good lad, Scamper! Good dog, then!'

Peter's father was standing by, very much amused by all this. 'Well – when we've all finished saying nice things to each other, I think we'd better go in,' he said. 'It will soon be supper-time. Hello – who's this?'

There was a clattering of hooves, and a pony-cart drew up outside the front gate. 'Whoa!' said an enormous voice.

'It's Mr Dinneford!' said Janet, in a fright. 'Oh, Daddy, Daddy – DON'T let him take Brownie away, will you?'

'Of course not. Go indoors,' said her father. 'Both of you. Look out of the window if you

like, but no listening. You stay here, Tolly.'

The children fled indoors and pulled a curtain so that they might look out and see what happened. Oh dear – how dreadful if Brownie was taken away!

They could hear loud voices, but couldn't understand a word. The three men were very angry.

'Tolly! What do you mean by stealing my horse?' shouted Mr Dinneford.

'You said you were going to shoot him, so he

was as good as dead, wasn't he?' shouted back Tolly. 'I'm not going to let a good horse like that be shot, even if he *has* got useless hind legs.'

'Useless! You're about right there!' yelled Mr Dinneford. 'Why should I keep a useless horse, eating his head off in my stables? He's *my* horse, isn't he? Can't I do what I like with my own horses?'

'Within reason, Dinneford, within reason,' said Peter's father. 'But *you* need horses that are strong enough to pull very heavy loads – and that horse will never pull loads again. He will be quite useless to you. Why don't you sell him for what you can get?'

'How do you know he's useless?' yelled Mr Dinneford, angrier than ever.

'Well – we had the police vet here just a little while ago,' said Mr Tolly. 'And I'm afraid he didn't give a very good report.'

'What did he say?' asked Mr Dinneford, rather taken aback to hear that the police vet had been along. He wondered if Mr Tolly had told the police that he, Mr Dinneford, had proposed to shoot the horse.

'He said that the horse was nervy, because of his accident,' said Mr Tolly, 'and wouldn't be a bit of use to anyone for some time. He said you wouldn't get more than one hundred and fifty pounds for him now.'

'One hundred and fifty pounds! And I paid three hundred!' shouted the exasperated Mr Dinneford. 'And who'd give me one hundred and fifty pounds for him like he is now, tell me that!'

'Well – maybe he'll be better in a few months' time,' said Mr Tolly, 'and then . . .'

'Oh, don't tell me fairy stories about that horse! Those hind legs will *never* get better – they'll get worse! I shan't even be able to get one hundred pounds for him, let alone one hundred and fifty, you know that!'

'I'll give you one hundred,' said Mr Tolly, unexpectedly. 'And that's because I'm fond of him and don't want to see him shot.'

'Well, you're a nincompoop if you think that horse is worth even *one hundred* pounds!' raged Mr Dinneford. 'I don't believe the police said the horse was worth a penny! He should be shot!'

'Right. If you don't want to sell him, take him away and go,' said Peter's father, in a stern voice.

Mr Dinneford swung round. 'Do *you* want to give me one hundred pounds for him?' he said. 'Are you stupid too, like Tolly here?'

'I may be,' said Peter's father, 'but it's worth one hundred pounds to be rid of you. Either go and take the horse with you – or leave it here and take this hundred pounds. But make up your mind!'

'All right. I'll take the money,' said Mr Dinneford, a little ashamed of himself as he saw Peter's father's disgusted face. 'Good riddance to a nuisance of a horse, I say. Thanks for the money. Good evening.'

He pocketed the money and away he went striding off, leaving the horse behind. It had been scared of the angry voices, and had gone to Tolly for comfort. 'Now, now!' he said, stroking the soft nose. 'He's gone. You won't hear his loud voice again. You don't belong to him any more.' And he led the horse to Peter's father.

'Well, Tolly – the horse is *yours*,' said Peter's father. 'That is – if you want him. I'll deduct ten pounds a week from your wages till the money is paid off. That be all right?'

'Oh yes. Thank you very much,' said Tolly, his face one big smile. He put his arm round the horse's neck. 'Well, my beauty! You belong to *me* now – or you will in a few weeks' time – say five weeks. Could you deduct *twenty* pounds a week from my wages for five weeks? That will clear the debt. Ha – a hundred pounds of very, very good horse! You wait till a few months have gone by, my beauty, and you'll be as good as ever you were! You'll be worth your weight in gold!'

'Very well, Tolly,' said Peter's father, smiling at the old man's joy. 'You'll be less twenty pounds a week till the debt is paid off – and then Brownie will be yours for keeps. And a fine horse he is too, except for those weak back legs. But they'll improve. He'll be a fine horse again before very long – and you deserve to have him, Tolly. Take him off now and bed him down in the stables. He'll be happy to have you fussing round him again, I've no doubt!'

CHAPTER SEVEN

Tolly and Brownie

As soon as the children saw that Mr Dinneford had gone off and that Tolly was leading the horse to the stables, they raced out of the house to him.

'Tolly! What happened? Is he yours? You said you hadn't enough money to buy him. Oh, isn't he a darling?'

Brownie nuzzled both children gently. He liked them very much.

'He's mine all right,' said Tolly, proudly, as he backed the horse into his new quarters. 'There you are, my beauty. You stay there awhile till we find some supper for you and some water. Ha – someone's put plenty of good straw bedding down for you. You'll be well off here, old horse.'

'Have you really bought him, Tolly? Was Mr Dinneford very angry? We heard him shouting,' said Janet.

'Yes. I've bought him – though he won't be really mine for five weeks,' said Tolly, rubbing the horse's long nose lovingly. 'Your dad's going to take twenty pounds a week off my wages till Brownie's paid for – one hundred pounds your father gave for him – but *I* wouldn't sell him if you offered me five hundred!'

'Don't forget that you promised us we could have half of him for our own,' said Janet. 'We shall give you our share of the price as soon as we can. We've got some money in our money-boxes, and Granny is coming next week – she always gives us about five pounds each.'

'Now don't you worry about the money,' said Tolly. 'You don't *need* to pay me a penny for your share of him. I'll willingly share him with you. It isn't often children love horses like you two. You deserve half of my Brownie!'

Brownie was very pleased with his new stable. He threw back his head and sent a loud, delighted whinny through the whole place. The two other horses who were there were startled, and said 'hrrrrumphs' in surprise.

'He'll be pleased when he goes out into the fields,' said Peter. 'I bet he'll gallop all over the place, and make friends with any animal there, horse, sheep or dog!'

'Your dad's been a really good sort over Brownie and Codger,' said Tolly. 'Well, I must go back to Mr Dinneford's and get all my things. Stay quiet now, Brownie. I'll be back to sleep with you tonight. Can't have anyone stealing you!'

He said goodbye to the children and went back up the hill to Mr Dinneford's farm. Now – if that Mr Dinneford started on at him about old Brownie, he'd tell him a few truths and see what he made of those!

But Mr Dinneford didn't come near Tolly. He was now wishing that he hadn't told him to go! Tolly was a fine, trustworthy worker. Whatever would he do without him?

I'll clear up everything, and leave it all shipshape! thought Tolly. I'll miss all the

horses – but there, my new master will have plenty of them for me to care for!

That night Tolly went to see that Brownie was safe and happy in his new stable. In the afternoon the old horse had been out in the fields, getting to know one or two of the other horses who were grazing there. Then he had brought beets to the yard in a cart – a very light cart indeed, which did not strain his back legs at all.

Tolly watched him, very pleased. 'Those back legs of yours are better even than last week!' he told Brownie. 'Now you be careful of them – and lie down in your stable as much as you can. Don't stand all the time – even if you *do* want to talk to the horses next to you!'

Brownie had given a happy little whinny, as if he had understood every word. He sensed that his master was happy, for some reason, and so he was happy too. He wondered why he was in such a strange place, but as long as he could hear Tolly whistling somewhere not too far off, he was content.

And now here was Tolly settling down on an old mattress in the empty stall next to Brownie. The old horse was delighted. He couldn't *see* Tolly there, but he could smell his familiar smell, and he was comforted to feel that Tolly was nearby, as he stood in his stall in the strange stable.

'Now I'm here, near you, old horse,' said Tolly in a low voice. 'Sleep well. Lie down in your straw. I'm here, close to you. Nice and warm, isn't it? Good night, Brownie. You don't need to be afraid of horse-thieves while *I'm* close beside you! And old Codger is here too, in the straw. Say good night, Codger!' And

Codger gave a small bark as if to say 'Good night! Sleep well!'

Codger was the first one out and about the next morning. He scrabbled out of the straw in the stall he had slept in, and went to lick his master's face.

'Don't,' said Tolly, sleepily. 'How many times have I told . . .' And off he went to sleep again before he could finish his sentence!

Codger looked up at the half-door that shut him and his master into the stall. Yes – he could just about jump it. He crouched – leapt as high as he could – and just failed to get over the half-door. Instead he fell back heavily on to Tolly who awoke with a jump and a shout.

'HEY! WHO'S THIS? THIEVES, THIEVES!'

'Wuff!' said Codger, in a small, scared voice. Oh dear – what had he done? Awakened his master, and made him think there were thieves about!

'You silly little idiot, Codger!' said Tolly, crossly. 'What did you jump on me for? It isn't time to get up. Now you've woken up the horses. Hark at them hrrrumphing! I'll have to get out of this stall and quieten them!'

So up he got and went from stall to stall, patting and stroking, trying to quieten the frightened horses. 'Anyone would think horse-thieves were about!' he grumbled, as the horses stamped and shuffled uneasily. 'Now just you lie quiet, Codger, and don't move so much as a whisker. I want to go to sleep!'

CHAPTER EIGHT

Next morning

WHEN PETER and Janet woke up the next morning they each remembered about Tolly, and how he had bought old Brownie. Janet lay and thought about it for a little while, and then she slipped out of her room, and ran to wake Peter.

He was so sound asleep that it was hard to wake him. She shook him and pummelled him, but he just gave little grunts and turned away.

'Peter! You *know* you're not as deeply asleep as all that!' said Janet, crossly. 'All right. I've a pin here and I'll just see if *that* will wake you.'

Peter sat up immediately! He was cross and frowning. 'What's the matter? Don't you dare to stick that pin into me, you horrible girl. It must be awfully early in the morning. What's the matter?'

'It *isn't* early. It's only ten minutes to breakfast time,' said Janet. 'Do get up. I want to be down early to breakfast, and to talk to you about calling a meeting of the Secret Seven. We MUST let the others know about Tolly and Brownie and Codger. We've done everything on our own so far, and we oughtn't to do any more without at least *tell*ing them!'

'All right. Call a meeting then. I'm going to sleep again,' said Peter, snuggling down under the bed-clothes once more.

'You really are a stupid, silly sleepyhead!' said Janet, crossly. She got off the bed. 'All right, I'll take you at your word. Go to sleep all the morning if you want to. *I'm* going to call a Secret Seven meeting myself, see. I'll go round IMMEDIATELY after breakfast and warn everyone. I'll tell them you're not feeling too good, and that I'll take the meeting, and be its head, instead of you.'

'You will NOT!' said Peter, fiercely. He flung off the bed-clothes so violently that they fell all over Janet and she was nearly smothered. 'Go

away, you horrid girl. I'll turn you out of the Secret Seven if you go on like this!'

Janet gave a chuckle and went off to her own room. Ah now – *now* they would be sure to have a Secret Seven meeting. How she loved them! There was quite a lot to report too. 'I'll take some of the chocolates that Auntie gave me last time she was here. And I'll ask Rachel for some of the ginger cake she made two days ago. It was an enormous one – there must surely be lots left! There's such heaps to talk about we'll *need* something to eat. We'll talk about Tolly – and Brownie – and how Daddy bought Brownie for one hundred pounds, and that half Brownie is ours – and Tolly is sleeping in the stable with Brownie and our other horses . . .'

There was still quite a while before breakfast and Janet scribbled as many Secret Seven notices as she could.

'IMPORTANT: *A Secret Seven Meeting will be held in our shed at ten o'clock sharp, to report further proceedings on the complaint that Bob Smith made at our last meeting. Please come, as plenty has happened. Bring sweets or chocolates or ginger beer if possible.*

Janet. Secret Seven Club.'

Peter was cross with her at breakfast, so she didn't say a word about the meeting. Soon Peter spoke to her commandingly. 'After breakfast we'll go and write those notes to the others. Hurry up. There's not much time if we want to hold it at ten.'

'My *dear* boy – *I* wrote all the notes while you were half-awake!' said Janet. 'I was afraid you might not wake up even for breakfast!'

'Don't be an idiot,' said Peter. 'How *dare* you write notes to the Secret Seven members without even asking *me* what you're to put.'

'Well – it wasn't much *good* asking you,' said Janet. 'You were so sound asleep. I just hadn't the heart to wake you properly, you looked so very peaceful. Still – I can tear the notes up if you like. Perhaps you *had* better write them, and dictate every single one to yourself.'

'No – no, don't tear them up!' said Peter, as Janet took up the little pile of notes. He was alarmed at such an idea. *He* didn't want to have to begin writing out the whole lot again himself!

'Well – will you take them round to the others then?' said Janet. 'I'll get the shed ready.'

'All right. I'll go immediately,' said Peter. 'I *would* like to go and see how Tolly and Brownie and Codger are first, though. I dreamed about

Brownie all night!'

'What did you dream?' asked Janet, with interest. Peter sometimes had very, very interesting and exciting dreams.

'I dreamt he ran away with Codger because thieves came,' said Peter. 'And please don't remind me of it because I shall be scared of it coming true.'

'Baby!' said Janet. 'Hurry up with your breakfast. I'll go and make the beds.'

Peter gobbled the rest of his breakfast, snatched up the notes Janet had written and tore off to deliver them. He saw nobody at all as he pushed them through each letterbox and rang the bell before trotting off again down the front path. He was home in record time, and went to find old Tolly. Janet rushed after him.

Tolly was helping to milk the cows, and looked very happy. The other men had made him welcome, and had admired Brownie so much that Tolly nearly burst with pride.

'How's Brownie?' asked Janet, smiling as the old man placed a bucket under another cow, to milk it.

'Brownie's fine!' said Tolly, as the good rich milk squirted into the pail. 'Fine! He likes being with so many other horses. He's perked up a lot, Janet. You go and say good morning to him. He'll be pleased to see you. He'll be giving you gallops on his back over the fields and hills before you know where you are!'

Janet went to see the old horse. His head was over the stall-door, and she opened it and slipped in beside him.

'Brownie! Did you have a good night? Are

you happy here? You weren't frightened, were you, the first night in a strange place?'

'Hrrrrrumph!' said Brownie, and pushed the girl gently with his nose. She rubbed her hand up and down it.

'I like you, Brownie. I like you. Your legs will soon be QUITE all right, won't they? I'm sure they will!'

The other horses now had their noses over *their* doors, waiting for Janet to come by. They all knew her, of course, and loved her. She was always gentle and loving to them.

A bell rang out from somewhere. 'That's the bell to say I'm wanted indoors!' she told the horse. 'I must fly. Did Tolly sleep with you last night? I've just been to say good morning to him.'

And away she went, her hair flying in the wind just like a horse's mane!

CHAPTER NINE

Another meeting

THE TWO children soon gathered up the things they wanted to take to the meeting-shed. Rachel had been very nice and had given them half the gingerbread cake. 'It wants eating up,' she said. 'It's getting a wee bit stale, but you won't mind that, *I* know. And here's an apple for each one of you. The gardener brought them in – he says they're only windfalls, but they'll be sweet.'

'Oh, thank you!' said Janet, pleased. 'I usually buy some sweets or something for the meetings, but I haven't enough time now – not till I find my purse anyway – and goodness knows where that's gone! Hurry up, Peter. I'm just going down to the shed. The others will be here in half a tick.'

'I'm just going to make a few notes,' said Peter. 'I think we ought to find out if anyone has got money in to help to pay the vet's bill. We ought to begin to pay some of it off. We promised we would.'

'Well, I've got fifty pence,' said Janet. 'I didn't earn it, though. I found it on our gravel path this morning. I only hope I can remember where I put it!'

'Lucky thing!' said Peter. 'I'm taking a collection this morning at the meeting, so you *could* put it in that. Every little helps.'

'I was going to, of course,' said Janet. 'And I've opened my money-box too. Mother said I could take half of what I had there, to help to pay the vet's fees, if I really wanted to. I said that I'd do anything to help poor old Tolly.'

'So would I,' said Peter. 'I'll get *my* money-box too. I wish I hadn't spent so much on bull's-eyes lately. But I've had several good books to read – and a bull's-eye is just right for a good book. It lasts and lasts!'

At five minutes to ten they were down at the shed. Clean writing-paper was there, a pencil and a pen and a rubber. Even a ruler, though Janet felt sure that Peter wouldn't want *that*! Their money-boxes were there too, each with their keys in them for unlocking.

'Gingerbread cake!' said Janet, putting a plate on the table. 'A bit stale, but what does that matter? And an apple each. These two are a bit bad, Peter, *we'd* better have those and give the good ones to the others.'

'Right,' said Peter. 'Oh, you've brought some of your chocs too. Good! Shut the door, quick. I can hear someone coming. It might be Susie, that tiresome sister of Jack's and we're not having her in!'

Knock-knock.

'Password!' shouted Peter and Janet together. A plaintive voice came from outside. 'Peter – Janet – is it *still* "Scamper" because if there's a new password, I've forgotten it.'

'Enter!' called Peter, and in came Pam, with Barbara close behind her. 'Hello!' said Pam, 'I *thought* we hadn't changed the password. Hello, Scamper! How do you like being a password?'

Scamper licked her bare legs, and sat down

by Janet. He liked these meetings. There were always titbits of some sort!

One by one the others came, and soon the meeting was complete. Bob was there too, looking very thrilled. 'Any news of old Mr Tolly?' asked Colin. 'I don't seem to have seen *any* of you at all. I've had to do a lot of swotting.'

'Now,' said Peter, 'I will declare the meeting open, and ask the members if they have anything to say. You will remember what we talked about at the last meeting, and how we were all going to try and help Mr Tolly in some way.'

'Let's tell *them* what's happened since the last meeting,' interrupted Janet.

'Yes, yes – do tell us,' said Pam, Jack and George all together, while Colin, Barbara and Bob nodded their heads. 'We're just bursting to know!'

'Well actually, quite a *lot* has happened,' said Peter. 'Old Mr Tolly brought his horse Brownie here to us yesterday, and it's in our stable now. That horrid Mr Dinneford was very, very angry with Tolly. He said that Tolly had ruined the horse's back legs, and . . .'

'Oh – is the horse *here*?' said Pam, in excitement, and Peter frowned.

'Don't interrupt when I'm speaking,' he said. 'I'm the head of the Secret Seven, aren't I?'

'Ooooh, sorry, Peter,' said Pam, going very red. 'It's just that I so badly wanted . . .'

'Be quiet! Sh!' said everyone, and Pam sank back into her chair, half sulky.

'Where was I now?' said Peter. 'Oh yes – when the police vet came, he said that the horse's legs were quite badly damaged and that he was in a very nervy state – but that with gentle handling and kindness, he might be quite all right again in a few months' time. He said his legs were to be rubbed with some kind of stuff – Janet knows more about that than I do – she's done a little of the rubbing because she has gentle hands. And that's about all.'

'Oh *no*, Peter – you've forgotten the most important part – about *buying* the horse!' said Janet. 'That's what we want the *money* for!'

'Why – do you want the horse to belong to *every*body in the Secret Seven Club, instead of just us and Tolly?' said Peter. 'That's silly.'

'No, it isn't silly!' said Barbara, who was fond of horses. 'I'd just LOVE to think I owned part of a horse. I once owned half a dog. I and my cousin, who lived next door, shared it between us – we each put down half the money. I really do think that the dog *liked* being shared. I'm sure Brownie would. Think of having *seven* people spoiling him instead of just one. What a wonderful time he'd have! Fancy the Secret Seven owning half a horse! I bet no other club in the world does that!'

'Where *is* this horse?' asked Colin. 'I didn't see him when I came past the stables. They seemed empty to me!'

'Somebody must have stolen him then!' cried Janet, jumping up. 'Or left the door open. Peter, did you?'

'No! I haven't been *near* the stables!' said Peter, jumping up too. 'Oh – Oh, gosh – just look!'

And, as they all turned towards the open window of the shed, they saw a very, very pleasant sight. Brownie was putting his long nose inside! He had somehow got out of his

stall, and had heard the sound of voices, and come to investigate! What a lovely thing he looked, staring shyly in at the window. 'Hhrumph!' he said, in a mild, inquiring voice.

'He wants a piece of gingerbread!' said Pam, and would have given him the whole lot if Peter hadn't snatched the plate from her!

'The meeting is put off for half an hour,' said Peter, desperately. 'We really *can't* have Brownie at a meeting. STOP barking, Scamper. Oh goodness – there they go together, tearing over the lawn. *Look* at those hoofmarks! Now we're in for trouble!'

It took some time to capture the excited

Brownie. *He* thought that it was a wonderful game of 'Dodge About' and 'Don't be Caught' and he darted here and there, over flower beds and vegetable beds and lawns to his heart's content. The gardener and Tolly caught him at last, and led him firmly back to his stable.

'I'm ashamed of you, Brownie!' said the panting Tolly. 'Right – Down – Ashamed – Of You! I'll be working all day long on the beds you've trampled!'

'We'll help!' said the children, and they did. Tolly was very thankful to see the garden more or less itself again before Peter's father came out!

'We were in the middle of a Secret Seven meeting,' said Peter to Tolly. 'I suppose you couldn't come to it now, could you? – we're going to hold the rest of it immediately – in the shed – and we'd like you to tell us a few things.'

'Right,' said Tolly. 'I've got about a quarter of an hour to spare. What meeting is this?'

'We were going to discuss money,' said Peter, leading everyone back into the shed. 'You see, we have promised to pay the vet's fees for

Brownie – and we've got some money towards them this morning – and we also want to discuss the *buying* of Brownie.'

They were now all sitting round the shed, looking eagerly at the surprised Tolly. He gazed at the various money-boxes on the table, and at one or two envelopes and purses.

'That's what we've got already towards the vet's fees,' said Pam. 'That's my purse. I weeded my granny's garden for a day and a half, and she gave me five pounds! So *that's* to go towards the vet's fees.'

'And I took care of our neighbour's dog for two whole days while he was away,' said Jack. 'Awfully nice dog too, it was. *I* didn't take it walks. It took *me* walks! And guess what old Mr Kay gave me for that. He gave me two pounds fifty at first – and then when he heard what I was going to do with it – help with the vet's fees, of course – he trebled the money and gave me *seven pounds fifty* pence!'

'Good *gracious*!' said everyone.

'I'm afraid I wasn't so lucky,' said Colin. '*I* took *two* dogs for walks, but one jumped into a very dirty part of the river, and it came out absolutely *covered* with mud. So I'm afraid I only got one pound fifty – *and* I had to give the dog a bath too!'

'Bad luck,' said Peter. 'What about you, Barbara?'

'I brought my money-box. I think it has about nine pounds in it,' said Barbara. 'I had to buy rather a lot of birthday presents – three lots in three weeks – and the last one was two days ago. I'm sure there's only nine pounds in it now.'

'Bad luck. Never mind, you can always save up a bit more later on', said Peter. 'We shan't be able to pay much of the vet's bill *this* time. George, what about you?'

'Ha!' said George. 'I've got some NEWS. Some weeks ago I went in for a competition for an essay about clubs – the first prize was one hundred pounds and . . .'

'You surely didn't win THAT!' shouted Peter, standing up in excitement.

'No, no, I didn't win the first prize of one hundred pounds – but I *did* win the second prize – and that was *fifty pounds*!' said George, his face glowing. 'I heard this morning. I haven't got the money yet, but Dad says it will come all right. He gave me the fifty pounds in advance, so that I could give the whole of it to the vet for his fees for Brownie. I shall give the money back to Dad when my prize money arrives.'

There was a silence. *What* a wonderful thing to do! *What* a gift! Good old George! Now he was being hugged by Janet, and patted on the back by the others!

'Did your parents *say* you could give it towards the vet's fees?' asked Peter.

'Yes. I told them, of course. They were frightfully pleased,' said George. 'In fact, Dad nearly gave me *another* fifty pounds to match this one. Mother just stopped him in time!'

The gifts from the others didn't seem very exciting, after hearing about George's magnificent prize of fifty pounds! Peter put in his money-box savings, which amounted to seven pounds fifty and Janet put in hers, which came to four pounds altogether. Bob shyly put in four pounds fifty. 'Mostly for errands,' he said.

'How much does it all amount to?' asked Pam, eagerly. 'It looks an awful lot of money now it's out on the table. Enough to pay a dozen vets!'

Peter solemnly and slowly counted the collection of money on the table, including, of course, the exciting, crisp fifty-pound note!

'We have here the large sum of eighty-nine pounds,' he said. 'There!'

Jack lost control of himself in his excitement,

and jumped up, cheering so loudly that Scamper fled out of the shed with his tail well down!

'HIP HURRAY! HIP, HIP HIP, HURRAY!' And, of course, everyone joined in, including Tolly, who was almost as excited as the children.

'We've got enough for the vet's fees!' cried Peter, in delight. 'Oh, George – you *are* a brick to put in that fifty pounds! We'll never, never, forget that. NEVER! What a happy ending to a WONDERFUL meeting! HURRAY!'

CHAPTER TEN

Off to see the vet

TOLLY HADN'T said a single word. He had sat open-mouthed, listening to the excited children in the greatest wonder. He kept staring at the fifty-pound note on the table as if it was the first time he had ever seen one. Then he looked from one to other of the children with admiration and gratitude.

'I think we'd better explain things to Tolly,' said Peter, at last. 'We're all getting too excited – and Tolly must be wondering what all that money is doing on the table! Even Scamper's excited! SIT, SCAMPER. Will you please SIT?'

'Well, young man – I can't say that I'm used to seeing fifty-pound notes lying about,' said

Tolly, with a wide grin. 'That looks as if it's just come straight from the Mint, it's so clean and new.'

'Anyway,' said George, proudly, 'it's for paying the vet's fees for Brownie. Or it *could* go towards buying him.'

'What's all this about buying him?' asked Tolly. 'I'm having twenty pounds a week docked off my wages for five weeks – and then he'll be mine. I said Peter and Janet here could share him, seeing that they live here, and can look after him sometimes. But he's *my* horse – *I'm* paying for him!'

'We thought that if you'd let us pay *part* of the money, we'd *really* feel he was partly ours. Which half of him shall we have?' Janet looked seriously at Tolly, and he laughed as he looked back at her.

'Now don't talk ridiculous,' he said. 'You can't buy a horse in two halves. We'll each share the whole of him, and I'll be pleased to think you've a share of his love. I never did see such a loving horse before. Why, I believe he'd work his heart out for his owners!'

'Well, Tolly, listen,' said Peter. 'We shan't

feel as if we're *really* sharing him if we don't pay part for him – all the club members think the same. We'd all like to feel that we've shares in such a lovely horse. But we know he's *really* yours! Just let's share him a *bit*!'

'Right,' said Tolly, understanding at last. Of course! None of these children actually had a horse of his or her own – and they longed to have even a small share in one. Tolly understood that. Yes, he understood that. He nodded his head and gave the children a wide grin.

'All right, Peter. That's settled then. Pay me fifty pounds down, and you can reckon on your bit of him! And if you've any money left over, as I know you will have, then pay off a bit of the vet's fees – that would be really kind of you! I'll be a bit short for some weeks, paying over to your father for Brownie – and I can't manage the vet's fees too.'

'I tell you what!' said George. 'Let's pay half the vet's fees, and then just hand over what's left to Mr Tolly, to tide him over a bit. *We* don't want the money. The Secret Seven don't owe anything to anyone – and we can always earn a

bit more if we want to by doing odd jobs for our parents. And there will be birthdays coming along soon.'

'I wonder when *Brownie's* birthday is,' said Pam. 'If we have any money left over we could buy him a whole bag of carrots. When's his birthday, do you know, Mr Tolly?'

'That's in about ten days' time,' said Tolly, screwing up his eyes as he tried to remember. 'I've got it written down somewhere. A bit of a thing he was – all legs and head – a bonny wee horse, though. Now look at him – as fine a horse as ever I did see!'

'I think we might as well go and visit the vet today,' said Janet. 'We'd just have time to catch him before he goes out on his rounds. Shall we go?'

'Yes,' said Peter. 'We'll have time to go to his place, talk to him, and get back to finish our meeting. We'd better take the money with us. I do hope to goodness we've got enough. Come on, Scamper!'

They said goodbye to Tolly, and set off to the vet's house with Scamper trotting beside them. They were lucky. He was *just* going out after having seen his surgery patients, and was on his own fine horse.

'Hello, Mr Whistler,' said Peter, raising his cap. 'Can we speak to you just for a minute? You don't need to dismount. My, isn't he a fine horse?'

'Yes. He's a grand fellow,' said the vet, patting the horse on his neck. 'His name's Lord Lofty – suits him, doesn't it?'

'Yes!' agreed the children, also patting the great horse. And Pam added, 'He *is* lordly –

look at the way he holds his head aloft, and see how proudly he paws the ground. I'll bring you some sugar lumps next time I come, Lord Lofty, and kneel and present them to you on a silver plate!'

That made them all laugh. 'Well!' said the vet. 'Now what can I do for you? I'm just off on my rounds, and can only stop for a moment.'

'It's just that we've saved up the money to pay your bill for the horse called Brownie,' explained Peter. 'You know it – Mr Dinneford had it – a lovely brown horse with a beautiful head. Mr Dinneford sold it to my father, and now my father has sold it to Tolly, who's left Mr Dinneford, and is now working for my father. Rather a long explanation, I'm afraid.'

'Yes, yes. I know the horse well – he pulled a heavy cart downhill, and the cart pushed into his hind legs in some way, and injured them,' said the vet. 'I was angry with Dinneford over that – he always overworks his horses – uses two when he ought to use four! That horse suffered a lot – how are his legs now?'

'Well, *we* think they are a lot better, now

that Tolly's with us and looking after Brownie,' said Peter. 'And Tolly told us that you were a great help with old Brownie, and did a lot for him and his poor hurt legs. And we've come to pay the bill. You kindly said you would halve the fees, which is very good of you. So if you could tell us EXACTLY how much the bill is now, we thought we'd pay it, and then Tolly wouldn't worry about it any more. We've got enough money. We've all saved up – and George here, he won fifty pounds in an essay competition.'

'And he gave it towards your fees, and towards buying a share in Brownie. We're *all* going to share in Brownie,' said Colin, his face beaming. 'So he'll be jolly well looked after.'

'Well, I'm blessed! So *that's* what you've come for!' said the vet, smiling. 'Let's see now – my bill was pretty high – and I said I'd halve it – now look, I suppose you wouldn't like *me* to have a share in that horse, would you? I'm fond of him too, you know – and if I had a share in him, I could come and look after him for nothing if anything went wrong, couldn't I?'

There was a silence, as the children worked out what this meant. 'Er – well,' said Peter. 'Of *course* you could have a share in him too. You must be fond of him, seeing you've done such a lot for his poor old back legs. Yes, I'm sure Tolly would like you to have a share in him. But about your bill – if you could tell us what the half-payment is, we . . .'

'Good gracious – as if I should charge anything for looking after a horse in which *I* own a share!' said the vet, looking quite upset.

'But you *didn't* have a share when you attended him,' said Colin.

'Quite right. But I didn't know then that I was going to be lucky enough to be *allowed* a share in him, did I?' said the vet. 'No, no – you must let me have my way in this. Give me a share in the horse, and there'll be NO fees to pay for my attending Brownie when his legs were so bad. I wouldn't HEAR of it. Well, I must go. Good-bye – and pat Brownie for me, will you, and tell him that he's partly mine now, bless him!'

And with that the vet galloped off at top speed on Lord Lofty.

OFF TO SEE THE VET

'WELL!' said Peter, jubilantly. 'That's that. What a wonderful thing to happen! Good old vet – he's a sport! And to think that if Brownie gets anything wrong with him, he'll get free treatment. No big bills for Tolly to worry about. Why, Pam – what's the matter? What on *earth* are you crying for?'

'It's only just because I'm so happy, all of a sudden,' wept Pam. 'I don't know *why* I'm crying. I just can't help it. I'm so surprised and happy. Don't look so worried, Scamper. I tell you I'm very *happy*!'

All right, Pam. Everyone understands! Quite a lot of people would do the same, if they came across such unexpected kindness!

CHAPTER ELEVEN

Everybody's pleased

THE CHILDREN all went back to Peter's house as fast as ever they could. They could hardly believe their good luck! How kind of the vet! But how like him!

'I hope I'll be as generous as that when I grow up,' said George, solemnly. He had been very impressed with the vet's simple, heartfelt kindness. So money didn't count with some people, then? That was wonderful. Kindness mattered much more to the vet than even *pounds* of money. George never forgot that morning – and one day he was to grow up, and do the same kind of things – all because he talked to the vet about Brownie!

Tolly couldn't believe their good luck either,

when they burst in on him as he sat having his mid-morning snack, in the little old shed near the stables.

They slapped all the money down on the bench beside him – the fifty-pound note and the rest.

'The vet wouldn't take a penny!' said George. 'Not a penny. He said that all he wanted was a share in Brownie, he likes him so much and he'll come to see his legs for nothing! It's *true*, Tolly!'

'You're having me on!' said Tolly,

disbelievingly. 'That's what you're doing. Pulling my leg. Go on with you. You haven't been to the vet's! Have they, Scamper?'

It took some time to persuade Tolly that what they were telling him was the truth. Then he stood up, looking amazed. 'You mean to say that the vet didn't take a penny of your money?' he said. 'Not a penny? He's a gentleman, he is. A right-down, slap-up, true gentleman! And I'm going to take up to him all the eggs that my hen Sukey lays, every single one of them. He likes new-laid eggs – he told me he did. And he shall have Sukey's, if I go without eggs for the rest of my life.'

The children were amused by Tolly's outburst, and very pleased. Now the vet would have new-laid eggs every breakfast-time – and he certainly deserved them, everyone agreed on that.

'Funny how one kind deed leads to another, isn't it?' said Janet. 'Dear me – things have been very exciting lately. A bit *too* exciting. I feel quite out of breath. Oh well – I expect they'll quieten down now – but I must say I've enjoyed the last few days!'

Janet was wrong! They *didn't* quieten down! Instead they became very exciting indeed.

Peter went to tell his father what the vet had said, and Janet went with him. He listened without saying a word. Then when Peter came to the end of the story, he nodded his head.

'So he wouldn't take your money!' he said. 'Well, what are you going to do with it? It amounts to quite a bit.'

'We'd like to give it to you to pay for Brownie, so that Tolly can have him really and truly. He does so love him. Daddy – and after all, *he'll* be the one that has to look after him – we'll soon be back at school – and you're always busy. He'll be safe with Tolly and the other horses, won't he?'

'He'll be safe all right,' said Daddy. He gave them each a hug. 'Very well. I'll take the money, and it shall all be spent on Brownie – on his food, his stabling and everything. And maybe there'll be enough to spend on a good saddle, so that you can ride him. He'd like that.'

'Oooh – so would *we*! said Janet, at once, her eyes bright. '*I* know, Daddy – let him be *your* horse and Tolly's when we're at school – and *our* horse when we're on holiday. That's fair enough, isn't it?'

'More than fair!' said Daddy. 'Now you go and tell Mother all about this – I've some work to do out in the fields. I'll have a word with Tolly and tell him the arrangement we've made.'

'Well – that's fine!' said Peter, to Janet, as they went to tell their mother. 'I'll try to give Mother thirty pence a week for a supply of sugar lumps for Brownie. He gets some from Tolly too, so he'll be well off. Isn't he a nice horse, Janet – and to think we can ride him every day!'

Tolly was as pleased as anyone else about the new arrangement. 'Do Brownie good to have someone to ride him every day,' he said. 'He'll get fat if he doesn't get plenty of exercise. His kind of horse runs to fat very quickly. You can jump him, too, you know. He's a good jumper. You should have seen him leaping over the stream yesterday when a dog came barking round his ankles. I vow the dog thought he had wings! Anyway, he took to his heels and fled, and old Brownie, he stood grinning there on the other side of the stream, showing all his beautiful white teeth. I guess that dog thought he was going to be eaten up, when he caught sight of those teeth!'

The children laughed. Old Tolly knew how to tell a story all right! They followed him into the stables and sat down in the sweetly-smelling hay.

'Tell us a story, Tolly,' said Janet. 'You know such a lot of tales about the animals you've worked with.'

'No, no – I'm busy now,' said Tolly. 'These stables have got to be mucked out. Look, you take that fork there Peter, and give me a bit of help. You go and talk to old Brownie, Janet. He's along there, and maybe he'd like an apple out of the loft. And maybe you would, too!'

Soon Janet was sitting in Brownie's part of the stable, each of them munching apples. The horse gave a gentle little whinny, and nosed at Janet lovingly. The girl put her arms round his neck and smelt his nice clean horse-smell.

'I do like you, Brownie,' she whispered in his pricked ear. 'You won't get stolen, will you? I couldn't bear it. I'll look out of the window tonight to make sure there are no thieves about. It will be a clear, moonlight night, and I can see your stables from my bedroom. So don't feel afraid – I shall be looking out to see you're in no danger – or the other horses either. I'll send Scamper out to you if I see any thieves!'

CHAPTER TWELVE

In the middle of the night

EVERYONE WENT to bed early that night. Peter's father was tired for he had been helping with the farm-work, as one of the men was on holiday. Mother was always sleepy at night, and glad to go early. Only the children wanted to stay up to finish their books, but they were sent off to bed in spite of their complaints.

'And you're not to read in bed for hours and hours, see?' said Mother. 'You're to put out your lights in good time. Be good children, now.'

So off they went, grumbling. Their bedrooms were next to each other, so they could call to one another easily. They settled down with their books. Janet had a very, very exciting one, about smugglers' caves, and she read on and on, quite forgetting the time.

'You'll get a good scolding in the morning when you own up to the time you put out your light!' called Peter, putting his out. 'Good night, bookworm.'

Janet's book was certainly very exciting. She forgot all about the time. In fact, she forgot that she was in bed, she was so sure she was in the smugglers' caves with four children and their dog Timmy.

The clock downstairs struck very solemnly indeed. It was the big grandfather clock, and he had a deep, grave note. Janet listened, and counted. Good gracious – ELEVEN o'clock! Whatever would Mother say when she had to own up in the morning that she had heard old Grandfather strike eleven? Guiltily she put her book on the floor, put out her light, and drew back the curtain. At once the room was absolutely flooded in bright silver moonlight!

'How beautiful!' whispered Janet. 'Oh, how BEAUTIFUL! Just like extra lovely daylight with a sort of silver sheen.' She stood and looked out for a while, and then made up her mind.

I must go out in it, I must, I must! she thought. It's a fairy sort of night. I'll put on my dressing-gown and go and dance in the moonlight. I shan't tell anyone though – they'd think I was mad!

She pulled on her dressing-gown, called Scamper in a whisper from Peter's bedroom, and set off down the stairs. It all seemed very exciting, and not a bit frightening. The moonlight was so very, *very* bright!

She went out of the back door, and stood in the yard gazing up at the moon sailing along in the sky. It looked very big indeed.

I *can't* go back to bed when the moon is shining so beautifully! thought Janet. I know! I'll go and see if Brownie is awake! I'll whisper in his ear and tell him I've come to see him, because the moonlight is so bright. He'll be so pleased to see me.

She was afraid to walk round the yard in the moonlight just in *case* her mother or father happened to be awake and standing at the window to look at the moon. So she went quietly all round the yard in the shadows, Scamper close beside her.

And then Scamper suddenly gave a growl and stopped. He pulled at Janet's night-dress and gave another little growl. She stopped absolutely still in the dark shadow of a tree, and listened. What was Scamper growling at? A rat? A mouse running into its hole? She could hear no sound at all, and see no mouse or rat. So on she went again, still keeping in the shadows.

And then she heard a noise. It sounded like an exclamation – somewhere in the stables. Who could be there? Well, Tolly, of course. He always bedded down in straw or hay in the stables, his old mattress beneath him. He couldn't bear to leave his beloved horses!

Janet's heart began to beat very loudly indeed, and very fast. She put her hand on Scamper's collar, and whispered in his ear. 'Don't bark or growl. Keep close to me. I'll find out what's going on. I'll peep in at one of the stable windows. Now be quiet, Scamper, be quiet!'

Together they kept in the shadows and came to the big stables. The horses were restless, and were stamping their feet and moving about. One gave a little whinny.

And then a great noise sprang up! At least, it seemed a great noise to Janet, crouching in the shadows! There were shouts – yes, shouts in Tolly's voice. There were excited whinnies. There was the sound of men's feet. Then Tolly's voice came, 'HELP! HELP!'

Janet could now see into one of the stable windows. She looked down into the stables, and saw a fight going on. There were three men there, one holding Brownie, one holding another horse, and the third fighting poor Tolly! Crack! Bang! Biff! What a fight. Janet was terrified and couldn't help giving a scream. Tolly heard her, but the others didn't. He called out to the frightened girl peeping down at the fight from the window just above him. 'Get help quickly! Save the horses!'

'No good calling for help, old man!' said one of the thieves, roughly. 'There's no one near these stables!'

Janet, really frightened, raced back to the house in her dressing-gown and slippers. 'DADDY! MUMMY! Quick, the horse-thieves

are there! Tolly's fighting them! Daddy, DADDY!'

Her father and mother awoke at once, and her father raced downstairs in his pyjamas. When Janet ran into the house, her mother was already telephoning the police!

She sobbed out about Tolly being attacked, and her mother comforted her. 'The police will be here in a minute,' she said. 'You go into the drive and wait for them, and take them to the stables. I must go and see if I can help your father!' And, taking a large kitchen poker with her, she fled outside in her dressing-gown. How brave! thought Janet, proudly, waiting in the drive. Oh dear – why doesn't Peter wake up!

Just then the police drove up in their car. 'Hey, Miss – where's the fuss? Quick, tell us!' called a voice, and a big, strong policeman ran up to her.

'I'll take you,' cried Janet. 'Someone's stealing our horses. I saw them. Daddy's gone to stop them and Mother's gone too.'

What with shouts and yells, and whinnies and barks, a tremendous noise was coming from the stables! Janet began to tremble, but she bravely trailed behind the police in her old dressing-gown! Were her mother and father all right? What had happened to Tolly? Were the horses hurt – or Scamper?

She didn't want to go to the stables to see what was happening, but she had to. Good gracious, what a turmoil!

There was Daddy firmly on top of one horse-thief. And there was Tolly on top of another, hitting him well and truly. And dear me, there was a third one, down on his knees in front of Mother, begging her to let him go!

Codger and Scamper were having a simply wonderful time. They kept darting at the men and snapping at them, and the men were scared stiff. All the horses were upset and excited, scuffling and stamping and whinnying in their stalls. Janet felt as if she simply must sit down. Everything was *much* too exciting. So she sat on the cold stone wall outside the stables and waited for the fight to die down. Good gracious – WHAT a thing to happen! Oh, poor Peter – he was in bed, out of all this excitement. She really, really, must fetch him!

CHAPTER THIRTEEN

What an excitement!

JANET DECIDED to go and get Peter before all the excitement was over. He'd never, never forgive her if she didn't. So she flew upstairs at top speed, and shook him awake. 'Peter! Come quickly! We've got horse-thieves in the stable! Tolly fought them, and now the police are here and Daddy and Mother and everybody's fighting in the stables!'

'Don't be silly! You've just had a bad dream!' said Peter, astonished and cross. 'Go back to bed. Fancy waking me with a silly story like *that*!' And he turned over to go to sleep again. Janet shook him hard.

'Sit up, sit up!' she shouted. 'Then you can hear the row. You'll miss all the excitement.

Anyway, I'm going to watch from the window!'

By this time Peter began to think there might be something in what Janet was shouting about. So he leapt out of bed and ran to the window with her. Good gracious! What a row – what shouts – what biffs and scuffles – what barks from Scamper and excited neighs from the horses!

'Come on!' said Peter, and without waiting to put on his dressing-gown or slippers he fled downstairs, out into the yard, and into the stable. Whew, *what* an excitement!

Most of the trouble was over now. But what a fight it had been! Tolly had gone for the thieves with a pitchfork, and made them dance in pain. They had tried to let out the horses, but the brave beasts had stood their ground, and Brownie had done quite a bit of snapping and kicking. The men were terrified of him. He had got one of them into a corner, and the man did not dare to move, and was glad when a sturdy policeman came up to handcuff him! 'Take that horse away from me,' begged the man. 'He's just about broken my ankle with a

kick, and I wouldn't be surprised if he's bitten my ear off.'

'I hope he *has*,' said the policeman, grimly, and pushed the man roughly into the next stall, where two other men had also been imprisoned. One had been kicked on the arm, and was nursing the wounded limb, his face angry and fierce. The third man had been knocked down when Tolly had flung himself on him, and had a badly cut head.

'Are the horses hurt?' Janet asked Tolly, who, breathless with the fight, was standing holding on to one of the thieves.

'No – not hurt at all,' panted Tolly. 'Old Brownie's enjoyed the shindy. My, my – the way he pranced about, and kicked out with those big hooves of his! I began to feel sorry for these horse-thieves! I was knocked down once, but old Brownie came up and almost snapped the man's arm off. Good old Brownie. He wasn't a bit afraid. He was clever too. He never so much as snapped at a policeman – only at the thieves!'

With a lot of shoving and pushing the horse-thieves were taken to the police cars. They were difficult to handle, and, to Peter's delight, he saw that every thief had a good stout policeman sitting down hard on him. There certainly would be no escape for *them*!

'Everything seems very quiet suddenly,' said Mother. 'My word, what an adventure! What a good thing you were awake, Janet, and heard the thieves.'

'Er – well, actually I was still reading,' confessed Janet. 'And the moonlight was so lovely I decided to go out in it with Scamper – and heard the noise in the stables. Are you hurt, Tolly? Fancy – you *thought* horse-thieves might be coming some night, and you were right. What a good thing you sleep with the horses!'

'I wouldn't sleep anywhere else if I knew horse-thieves were about!' said Tolly, brushing himself down.

The horses were restive and uneasy. 'I think, if it's all right with you I'll take them all out for a quiet walk,' said Tolly. 'Then they'll probably settle down quietly for the rest of the night.'

'Right, Tolly. And thanks for all your help tonight,' said Peter's father. 'I'll see you get some reward for it. It's good to have a man like you on the job.'

'Tolly – what exactly happened?' asked Janet, excitedly.

'Well, I bedded down in the straw on my old mattress, in the stall next to old Brownie, see? And the horses, they went to sleep, seemingly, because I didn't hear much stamping or whinnying. And then, some time later on, old Brownie here he whinnied right in my ear – leaned over my stall and whinnied, he did. Quietly, as if he wanted to whisper.

'Well, I sat up, of course, and there he was

looking down at me anxiously. The moonlight was shining into the stable and it was as bright as day. Then I heard another noise – and that wasn't a noise made by any horse. It was a man sneezing, and trying to stop his sneeze. And I thought to myself, Oho, Here we go! Horse-thieves, or I'll eat my old cap!'

'What then?' asked Janet, breathlessly, her heart still beating fast.

'Well, then up I get, push open the half-door, and stand up to see what was what. And I saw a man undoing the latch of Major's stall, up there, see. And old Major he began to carry on alarming. He snorted and whinnied and stamped till I thought he'd bring the stable down. How that man got him out of his stall, I don't know – but I do know that as soon as Major had room to kick out, he did – and that fellow went flying from one end of the stable to the other! Then I saw more chaps and I went mad. I picked up that there pitchfork and they struggled with me like madmen. They didn't want to get pricked by that sharp old fork. But there's one of them won't be able to sit down for a fortnight, that he won't!'

And old Tolly went off into a hoot of laughter that made all the horses turn round and look at him.

'Go on, Tolly. This is a tale worth telling,' said Peter's father, looking grim and amused at one and the same time.

'I don't really know what I did next,' said Tolly, scratching his head. 'I do know I saw one of them with my old Brownie again, and I caught hold of Brownie's head, swung him round and told him to kick the fellows out – send them flying. And old Brownie, he's always obedient, you know. My word, he sent two of them flying! One cracked his head on a door – and didn't he howl! "Shame on you," I said. "You'll wake up all the bobbies in the district" – and bless me, at that very minute the police came and joined the fight. Like magic, it was!'

'Well, you've done a grand and a brave job tonight, Tolly,' said Peter's father. 'I hope you'll regard yourself as on my permanent staff now – head of the stables – and over any of the younger staff. I can do with a man like you here! Why that fellow Dinneford let you go, I don't know! Well – see to the horses for a while and quieten them and then bed down yourself. Good night.'

And with that he put his arm round his wife's shoulders, motioned to the two excited children to go on in front and shepherded everyone back inside the house, including a most excited Scamper.

'How any of us are going to sleep tonight, I don't know!' he said. 'Too exciting for words! Well – we'll talk about it in the morning – and now – good night, Peter, good night, Janet. Sleep well!'

The children didn't want to go back to bed. They wanted to stay and talk and talk about all that had happened. They wanted to go and speak to each of the horses, they wanted to talk to Tolly – in fact, they wanted to do anything but go to bed.

But their father was determined. 'I said "Go back to bed" and I meant it. You'll catch frightful colds staying out here with so little on, after being in warm beds – and you're missing your night's sleep. If you don't go back to bed straight away now I shall forbid you to go near Tolly *or* the stables tomorrow, and that you won't like at all!'

'All right, Daddy – we're going,' grinned Peter. 'Goodness, what a night! I've never had an adventure like *this* before – in our very own home. What in the world will the other members of the Secret Seven say when we tell them tomorrow!'

'Off you go, for the last time!' said his father, giving him a firm push. 'Go and think about it in bed.'

At last the two children were safely in bed, shouting remarks to one another from their different rooms. Then suddenly Peter had no answer to his questions and knew that Janet was asleep!

Both children slept late when morning came, and didn't even hear the breakfast gong. Their mother let them lie in bed, remembering how late they had been the night before. But they were cross when they got up at last and found that quite a bit of the morning had gone. 'Oh, *Mother*! We wanted to go round and call the Secret Seven to another meeting!' grumbled Peter. 'They *must* know all that happened last night. It was so very, very exciting.'

'Will you please finish your breakfast and stop grumbling, Peter dear?' said his mother. 'You've the whole day to call a meeting. I shall clear away your breakfast in exactly ten minutes' time, so if you *want* a good breakfast you'd better get on with it.'

It was exciting to talk about the night before. Immediately breakfast was over they went to talk to Tolly. He was rubbing down one of the horses, whistling between his teeth. He grinned at the two children.

'Well – we had a night of it, didn't we?' he said. 'They nearly got my old Brownie! Ah, they didn't know how loudly he could hrrrrrrrumph! Woke me up at once, he did.'

'They didn't know that you slept in the stable with the horses, either, else they'd have been more careful,' said Janet. 'You're very fierce, aren't you, Tolly? I felt quite scared of you last night when I saw you with that hay fork.'

'I reckon *they* feel scared of me this morning too,' said Tolly, wringing out his cloth in the horse-pail. 'I keep thinking of that chap that won't be able to sit down for a week – and the other one, *he* won't be able to walk for a fortnight!'

'A jolly good thing too!' said Peter.

'Well, it's what horse-thieves deserve!' said old Tolly. 'I remember the last time I had to do with a horse-thief. He came stealing past my cottage into the stables I was in at that time, and I saw his shadow on my blind. Well, me and Codger, we got up at once, and I took my old pail with me – and I told Codger to chase the man to the old pump – and my, when I got there too, I worked the pump and filled my pail, and over the fellow's head went the icy-cold water. He couldn't get away – Codger saw to that – and I threw five more pails of water over him. Laugh! I had to sit down on the old wall to get my breath, I'd such a stitch in my side.'

Tolly knew how to tell a story very well, and the children could have listened for ages. But Tolly had work to do.

'Wait a minute, Tolly, wait,' said Peter. 'We're going to spend some of that money on a birthday party for Brownie, and all of us – you too – are to come. We'll get some very special oats for Brownie, and a whole pound of sugar lumps and . . .'

'Now look here, Peter, nobody's going to give my Brownie a pound of sugar lumps!' said Tolly, in alarm. 'He'd be as fat as an old cow in no time – and his poor back legs would have even more weight to carry. He . . .'

'It's all right, Tolly. We shall give *you* the sugar lumps to dole out to him!' said Peter. 'Or you can dole them out to us to give him. We promise not to make him fat. He's exactly right as he is!'

No notes needed to be written to call the Secret Seven to a meeting. When the news ran round Peterswood that horse-thieves had been to Peter's house, the rest of the members came rushing down to find out what had happened! Peter took them all down to the little meeting-shed.

The members sat down expectantly, all agog to hear everything. 'The milkman told *me*,' said Pam. 'And I rushed round and told the others – but most of them knew. Peter, what happened? Are the horses safe?'

'Perfectly,' said Peter. 'But I have a fresh piece of news for everyone. The night before they came to us, they went to Mr Dinneford's – and took his three *best* horses! And nobody knows where they are yet.'

'Serve him right,' said George, and the others nodded in agreement. 'Horrid man! Well, he lost Tolly through his bad temper and meanness – and now he's lost three of his horses. Will the horses be all right?'

'Oh yes – they are too valuable to be ill-treated by the thieves – they'll be all right except for a fright. But goodness knows where the thieves have taken them to – or who has bought them!'

'Well – I just *can't* feel sorry for Mr Dinneford,' said Peter. 'When I think how he spoilt dear old Brownie's hind legs through making him work with an overloaded cart, I just think to myself, "Well, serve him right!"'

'I think we all feel like that,' said Barbara. 'Peter, did you find out when Brownie's birthday is?'

'Oh yes – that's really what I wanted to call

a meeting about,' said Peter. 'It's on Friday. I've spoken to Dad about it, and he says he'd like to join in too, and make it a really good day for Brownie and Tolly. And don't you think we ought to ask Bob too? It was he who told us about Brownie and Tolly.'

'Yes – of course ask him – fine!' said George, and the others nodded in complete agreement.

'Dad says that he thinks it would be a good idea to spend most of the money we have left on helping to buy a decent saddle for Brownie,' said Peter. 'Then Tolly can ride him in comfort, and Brownie will love that. Dad also said that we must get a really good one, and so *he* will put some money towards the saddle too, as he feels so grateful to Tolly for saving our horses last night.'

'Good idea!' cried everyone, very pleased, and Colin added, 'Very decent of your father!'

'Well, there'll be plenty of money left for a super party,' said Peter. 'I vote we have it in the stable yard, so that all the horses can look out of the stable – and see us – and we can give them sugar lumps so that they can feel they're in the party too.'

'Hurray!' cheered everyone, getting really excited. 'Hurray!'

And that is why they are now all sitting down to a long table set out in the stable yard. Brownie's birthday has arrived. He is thirteen years old today, though he doesn't know it. He can't *imagine* why everyone is making such a fuss of him – and look at the garland of flowers he's wearing – doesn't he look fine! Dear old Brownie – everyone loves you!

Hanging in the stable is a fine new saddle,

just right for Brownie to wear. That's what Peter's father and the children bought for Tolly – and he's so proud of it that he can hardly wait to put it on Brownie's back and ride him.

There's a birthday cake too, with 'Happy Birthday, Brownie!' on it. Well, well – if ever a horse could be proud, Brownie could be today!

But he's not at all conceited. There he stands, look, his big brown eyes as kind as ever, his coat shining beautifully. Ah – sugar lumps! Good! And a slice of iced cake – even better! And a fine handful of the very best corn from Tolly's horny hand – a very nice titbit indeed.

'Hrrrumph, hrrrumph, hrrrumph!' says Brownie, and everyone laughs as Brownie nods his head politely.

'He says "Thanks, thanks, thanks!"' says Janet. 'Mr Tolly – I really do think he's the nicest horse in the world!'

'You're right there, Janet you're right!' said Tolly, taking Brownie another piece of cake, and look, Brownie is nuzzling into his ear, just as if he is whispering to the old man.

'He says he reckons there's no children like

you!' reported Tolly, and that made everyone laugh.

Well, I think Brownie's right, Secret Seven. I really do think he's right!